THE

EXPERIENCE

A Story of Aspergers and Aliens

By

Howard J. Levinson

The characters and events portrayed in this book are fictitious. The setting is in the St. Louis, Mo. region. Certain public institutions and public offices are mentioned. The characters and activities are imaginary. Any resemblance to actual events, locales or persons, living or dead, is entirely coincidental.

Prologue

The street lamps snaked past MarlonDale
Hendershat's house, just like they did on every
street in his subdivision and along every road in
the civilized world. Only a select group of young
people with Aspergers have the genetic imprint
to understand the threat these seemingly
innocuous illuminators pose to the continued
existence of every being on Earth.

The lights on MarlonDale's street were the
SilverLiner brand of Mercury Vapor lamps. Ten-
year-old MarlonDale Hendershat, (ten letters
first name, ten letters last name) watched as they
flickered to life. He sat in his webbed lawn chair
on his porch and watched and waited. Just as he
had done every twilight for as long as he could
remember.

The white light bathed his neighborhood.
And then it happened like it always did. The air
became dense, viscous and warm, very warm.
MarlonDale liked the warm, especially during
the bleak Missouri winter months. As soon as
the light steadied, it happened.

The concrete of the street roiled like angry ocean waves. It rolled back onto itself like a huge, chocolate HoHo, and whipped by at cartoon avalanche speed, disappearing towards the sundown. The smell following the street rollup was both astringent and pungent, a sharp, dank odor of fresh dirt and sulphur.

A singular, shiny being, surrounded by halogen white light, popped up from the ground like toast, directly in front of MarlonDale's house. Sparkles of yellow and silver trailed after it and then showered down on the dirt, twinkling and shimmering in the darkness.

MarlonDale thought this unusual. The aliens he was accustomed to viewing usually came in groups.

This being looked at him. That was unusual too. They never noticed him. He was always just a watcher.

The silvery being communicated in TenSpeak. Another "unusuality," MarlonDale thought. Only MarlonDale spoke in TenSpeak. He invented the language and as far as he knew, only he used it. TenSpeak, where every sentence contained ten words, and contractions counted as one. If only one word was spoken, it had to contain ten letters. TenSpeak required no conscious effort. It was just how he arranged his words. Tens, multiples of tens, decimals felt orderly and comfortable. Decimal, was comfortable.

MarlonDale liked shiny things. Shiny things were comfortable like decimals. He felt comfortable watching the shinies, as he had come to call them.

The alien spoke to MarlonDale telepathically. "You are one of the few who has been chosen. In time, you and two others will mend our worlds."

The being slipped silently back into the ground. The aura and sparkles whirled clockwise after it like water down a sink drain. MarlonDale was excited. He tapped his thigh vigorously with his thumb and little finger. He played "Wipe Out."

MarlonDale stared at the empty dirt street where the alien had appeared and disappeared. "I wonder who the other two world menders might be?"

He looked up at the street lamp and shook his head. "And everyone thinks they travel in space crafts, flying saucers."

MarlonDale has Aspergers, a behavioral disorder that has been getting some public mileage of late. It's been mentioned that Michelangelo, Benjamin Franklin, Thomas Edison, Teddy Roosevelt, Albert Einstein, Bill Gates, Woody Allen and Dan Akroyd have behavioral traits consistent with Aspergers. Dr. Temple Grandin, best-selling author of "As I See It," is an Aspie. Aspergers was first identified as a behavioral disorder in 1944, a relative newcomer to psychological ailments. It was not listed in the Diagnostic and Statistical Manual of Mental Disorders, the relative dictionary of mental illness, until the mid 1990's.

MarlonDale is an Aspie. His brain is wired differently. He can experience things, so called normal people cannot. As far as anyone knows, he is the only Aspie who has a personal relationship with aliens. This is his story.

Chapter 1

MarlonDale's father is Terry P. Hendershat, M.D. He is an infectious disease specialist at the Washington University Hospital Centers in St. Louis, Mo. Dr. Hendershat is responsible for a staff of 10-12, depending on the current budget, a gaggle of residents, and a laboratory he shares with some of the epidemiological specialists at the St. Louis University Institute for Bio-Security. The laboratory maintains a cache of some nasty little creatures of the viral and bacterial kind that they actively use in several federally-funded research projects.

Terry's personal stock value was quite average until the terrorist attacks on September 11, 2001. In the days following 9/11, Infectious Disease specialists became vitally important to national security. Anthrax, smallpox and plague, became everyday words.

Infectious Disease docs and public health personnel garnered real interest, followed by money for facilities, resources and research projects. Terry had been asking for an extra administrative assistant for two years prior to 9/11. He had his second admin by Thanksgiving 2001.

Terry Hendershat is the typical prototype of a physician researcher. Quiet, meticulous, orderly, asocial, and quite suspicious of the Washington University and Saint Louis University political machinations. He is tall and sinewy, displaying a curmudgeonly lankiness that pays little attention to fashion.

Every day he puts on a clean, short sleeve, white dress shirt and dark blue slacks. He wears one of his three tweed sport coats with suede elbows, even during the hot and steamy St. Louis summers. At the lab, the sport coat is hung on a coat rack, replaced by his lab coat, usually splotched with coffee and this morning's danish.

Terry has been known to sleep at his desk if a lab culture is nearing time for evaluation, but for the most part, he is a homebody. He enjoys his home, his garden and his deck overlooking a sloping backyard that joins a wooded area. The deer are problematic for his garden, but he likes to watch the gentle creatures as they tread lightly towards the house. The deer have eaten more vegetables from the garden than he has the last 2 years running.

Terry is aware that his eldest son, MarlonDale is very special. He had no idea how special.

Chapter 2

Mrs. Terry Hendershat is even more casual, eclectic, and idiosyncratic than her husband. Physically they are a striking pair. Margherite Hendershat is also tall, 5'9", but not gawkishly thin like her husband. She is full figured and wears flowered sun dresses all year around. The tags indicate that the dresses are made of hemp material by former followers of the Black Panther Party or Grateful Dead, handmade in the same area in San Francisco that produces Jerry Garcia ties. Margherite is a remnant from the Woodstock generation. She is the wife of a respected physician researcher and the mother of their two boys, Layton age 17 and MarlonDale, age 19. But first and foremost, Margherite is a poet, painter, sculptor, knitter, quilter, collector and writer. She is a woman who is occasionally depressed and prone to delusions.

Margherite was a student at the University of Missouri in rural Columbia, Mo., in the late 1960s. She majored in art and journalism. She was in grad school studying Mayan ceramics and Renaissance painters when Terry came into her life.

Terry was in his third year of medical school, working a night shift in the hospital's bacteriology lab. Margherite at the time had picked up a job in the hospital's library, re-shelving periodicals and reference journals. They met in a library aisle and 14 months later, walked down another.

Terry finished a residency in Infectious Disease at the UMC medical school and in 1980 they moved to St. Louis. Terry was offered a research position at Washington University's School of Medicine. Twenty seven years later, Terry is still there.

As soon as they settled in St. Louis, Margherite and Terry began planning a family. They did not use any birth control. After 9 years, they had yet to become pregnant. Margherite and Terry underwent a variety of testing, only to conclude that Terry's swimmers and Margherite's eggs were perfectly healthy. They could consider artificial insemination, but Margherite was adamant that she wanted everything normal.

Chapter 3

One spring morning in 1987, Terry awoke about 4 a.m.

"Margherite, wake up. Margherite," Terry sat up and shook his wife's shoulders.

"What, what is it, is everything alright?" Margherite asked.

"I just had a dream that was more real than any dream I have ever had. I can still taste the ocean salt and feel the water on my skin. Holy shit!" Terry said and did not stop rambling to allow Margherite to reply.

"We were on a cruise, I don't know, I didn't recognize the ports, but it was the Caribbean and we were deep sea fishing, a private boat, a Hatteras, yes, a Hatteras, I am sure of it, must have been at least a 40 footer. We were on deck fishing, it was warm and sunny as you would expect. A magnificent white cumulous cloud passed over the boat, obscuring the sun and it cooled off dramatically.

And then a voice from the clouds rumbled out like, I don't know, James Earl Jones or Charlton Heston. It was God-like. I must assume it was God talking to me," Terry paused.

"What did God tell you Terry, so I can get back to sleep," Margherite said, rolling onto her side.

"It, He, whatever, he said, 'You will have two sons, the first will be special, he will be yours, but know that I am always with him.' Margherite, the voice shook me awake. But I still heard it. Then he said, 'Your first born will be a leader. Your second also, but I will not be as close to him as the first. Be well to listen as I speak, as I am with you too.' Then the cloud vanished and the sun returned. It gives me chills just thinking about it. Margherite, what did I eat last night? Was the story of the Ten Commandments on TV or something?" Terry asked.

Margherite had gathered up her senses enough to focus on Terry and could see that he was now standing next to the bed, dripping in sweat. She scooted over to his side of the bed and made him sit down.

"Terry, you look really ill. Do you feel ok?"

"Yea, I mean, actually I feel energized," Terry said.

Terry took his pulse, which was duly noted to be taching out at 120 beats per minute and his respiratory rate was a pant at 24 per minute. Margherite returned from the bathroom with a moist towel and wiped off his forehead and chest. As Terry sat for a few minutes, his vitals returned to normal.

"I suppose I am no different than any other man, from the Biblical days to present. I guess I can have a vision like Moses or Abraham, right?" Terry asked, looking for some sense as he put on a dry T shirt.

"Yes my love….and those men were prophets you may recall. And there were some pretty difficult times when they came out of the prophet closet, weren't there?" Margherite suggested.

"Listen, I am not foretelling plagues or the end of the world or anything like that. I think we are going to have kids sometime. Maybe we should take a cruise and see what happens, what do you think?" Terry said as he slid his hand under Margherite's T-shirt and massaged her left breast.

"I am all about some sun and surf lover boy. But, I'm not getting any younger. My biological clock is ticking. We don't have to wait to book the cruise to work on making babies," Margherite said as she slid her hand under Terry's boxers and tugged them down to his knees.

Chapter 4

Terry's divine intervention dream did nothing to assuage Margherite's concern and that their first born would be special. Margherite was 38 years old at the time of her first pregnancy and she was concerned. In her hippie days, she smoked a lot of weed, ate some magic mushrooms, and on a few occasions, took a hit of acid. Even though it was years ago, she still worried. Margherite wanted to optimize chances for a normal baby and decided to have a natural child birth, no drugs.

MarlonDale, their first child, was born on January 1, 1988, 01/01/88, in a natural vaginal delivery without the accompanying drugs or procedures that could have offered some modicum of relief.

Marlon's birth took a little more than 30 hours of labor. Margherite continues to call that process her contribution to the acrimonious suffering women have been subjected to since Adam and Eve.

Their second child, Layton, was delivered 18 months later, under an epidural. Layton also was born without any complications. He and Marlon appeared normal, at least initially.

Chapter 5

Prior to the birth of their boys, Margherite and Terry had purchased an older three-story home in a private neighborhood of gated streets not too far from the university complex. As a young couple with only themselves to be concerned about, it was not overly disquieting that the area surrounding their exclusive streets could be a fairly dangerous zone, given the current gang-related crack cocaine wars. But their house had a turn-of-the-century "Meet me in St. Louis" stature, and it was very conveniently located to the hospital complexes that would serve to keep Terry employed. However, with the birth of their first child, the occasional gunshots and news of another murder three blocks away drove them to the suburbs.

In 1990, they moved into the house where MarlonDale would eventually meet his extraterrestrial friends. The home was located in a subdivision west of the city limits in the suburbs. The homes on their street all were located on ½-acre lots with manicured lawns and mature trees. It was a nice area for young families. The commute for Terry was an easy 30-40 minutes, which he managed daily in a respectable 1980 Volvo station wagon.

When they moved to St. Louis, Margherite took to poetry reading and art showings at the St. Louis Art Museum. In the years prior to MarlonDale's birth, she became known in the community of art patrons as a free spirit. Margherite combined her love of her own avant-garde poetry with her appreciation for renaissance period painting in a rather unique form.

Margheurite subscribed to an 18th century concept held by some of the more avant-garde Renaissance artists of the time. She believed, as did Alberti and Rodolfi that one could enter an altered state of consciousness through controlled body kinesics. The artists would hold long and static, often uncomfortable postures, and intersperse them with spasmodic, frenetic movements of the trunk and extremities. This see-saw of motion stimulated various parts of the brain, resulting in a fusillade of heretofore hidden creative images. These were immediately transferred to canvas. The paints mixed with the sweat and pain of the artist.

Margherite painted with kinetic passion and combined poetic readings with physical theatre. As the art critic from the *St. Louis Post Dispatch* wrote in a review, *"Margherite Hendershat conducted a reading of three of her poems last night in the gazebo above Art Hill during this week's 'Art on the Hill' confluence. At times, Mrs. Hendershat's poetry flows to the beat of a Ricky Ricardo conga drum immediately followed by the stillness of a cardiac flatline. The reading was the most physical and temporal display this writer has ever witnessed; She melds theatre, poetry, dance and art and is only seen when Mrs. Hendershat presents.*

Mrs. Hendershat appeared in a full length dress of a tight white weave muslin with puff sleeves and flounce cuffs, with a neckline that hung off her shoulders to give a hint of sexuality.

The overskirt was a dark maroon that was cinched up with eye hooks, once again adding that 'wench' sensuality. The long skirt followed behind her, billowing, as she gnawed and thrashed through her reading.

The reading concerned the difficulties that St. Francis of Assisi met during his life and the legacy left for those to follow. Her presentation included an on-stage, life-sized El Greco painting of the saint.

Mrs. Hendershat hurled her words with volume, engaging tonality and spittle, flailing and thrusting around and about the painting. Mrs. Hendershat successfully developed intersecting points between the artistic representation by El Greco, and her poetry, defining the relationship between the positional sense in art, the proprioceptive vision of the artist and subject and the intimacy of painting in the moment. The reading ended as Mrs. Hendershat removed the painting from its stand, leaned against the foremost leg, extended her arms in a Christ-like position and exhaled deeply in a long a raspy death rattle, signifying in her own last words 'all life ends.' "

Terry was supportive of his wife's eccentric behavior, attended her shows, and nurtured her needs, sending her to Europe on occasion to visit museums and do 'research'. All this before MarlonDale was born. With a baby on board and then two sons, Terry expected that Margherite would settle down and try her hand at motherhood.

Margherite settled somewhat, taking MarlonDale with her when she gave readings or attended other artist's presentations. She included MarlonDale in a few of her displays, dressing him in silly baby renaissance clothing and placing him in copies of wooden cribs circa 1600. With the birth of Layton, Margherite entered a period of melancholy which she managed with Bloody Mary's and Cosmopolitans.

Chapter 6

Margherite became concerned when MarlonDale avoided making eye contact with her. Bath times, diaper changing, feeding and playing seemed essentially normal activities, except he would not look her in the eye. She tried everything, even tricks. When sitting directly in front of her, the spoon on the way to MarlonDale's open mouth, his eyes focused on the incoming applesauce airplane, Margherite would put her head in the path of the spoon and, like a light switch, Marlon's eyes rolled up and away to avoid contact. He had other odd behaviors. He would fixate on anything reflective or shiny. Any toys not shiny, were ignored.

Terry and Margherite discussed the differential diagnostic possibilities ranging from Autism, Fragile X syndrome and a variety of other developmental disorders. Marlon was poked, prodded and scanned. He was videotaped at a daycare center. Childhood behavior specialists and a couple of neurologists could find no organic cause for Marlon's failure to make eye contact and quirky play activity.

They recommended that Terry and Margherite monitor MarlonDale's activities as he started school and try to continue a normal socialization process within and outside the family.

Layton, had no problem with eye contact and played with all of his toys, shiny or dull. Layton and MarlonDale interacted well and for a few years everything seemed fine.

Terry and Margherite were satisfied that MarlonDale was special in some fashion and they would deal with it during school years. Special, as advertised in Terry's dream.

One of the stranger behaviors MarlonDale exhibited at around age 5 was his TenSpeak. Every sentence contained ten words, conjunctions counting as one. One-word responses always contained ten letters. The only exception was when he sang songs out loud. He became particularly fascinated with the song "Big Rock Candy Mountain."

MarlonDale sang "BRCM" every morning while getting dressed, and every evening just before dusk, since he was a little boy. The song concerns a faraway mystical land where desires, dreams and needs are met: a Utopia.

Days and weeks, months and years passed by, mechanically as an escalator. MarlonDale was 10 years old at the time of his first telepathic Mercury Vapor Experience with aliens. He had sung Big Rock Candy Mountain 730 times per year, every year.

Chapter 7

MarlonDale's peculiar behavior had become increasingly obvious as he entered his pre-teen and teenage years. Terry believed it probably was in some fashion, hormonal. Margherite found some comfort in the fact that her son was special. That he was eccentric, more like her, a free spirit. But, as MarlonDale's behavior became more peculiar, Margherite experienced increasing anxiety and depression.

MarlonDale clearly exhibited behavior that had to be classified as more than free spirited. He put his clothes on in a specific order. Left sock, right sock, right pants leg, left pants leg. Both arms had to enter his shirt at the same time. He laid the shirt on his bed and wriggled into it. Shoes were put on last. The right then left.

Despite the odd behaviors, MarlonDale functioned well enough to maintain a B average in school. Their own doctor and the school counselors said to give it some time, so they did. Terry and Margherite were busy with their lives, hoping MarlonDale would develop out of it, in typical parental blinder fashion.

His TenSpeak, while cumbersome to others, was fully developed and automatic.

"MarlonDale, what are you going to do today?" Terry would ask at the breakfast table.

"I am going to go to the store with mom," MarlonDale would answer.

"Which store?"

"I think we are going to the grocery store first."

Terry would play games in an attempt to get MarlonDale to engage in longer sentence structure, but was unsuccessful.

"MD (MarlonDale's nickname), do you think you could tell me the route, name the streets and which way you will turn to get there?" Terry would ask.

"We will turn out of the driveway and go right. We will be going south on Appalachian Way one mile. We turn left on Olive Boulevard and go two miles. We will turn left into the Whitehall Mall and park. And the ZIP code for Whitehall Mall there is 63017." MarlonDale answered in clipped sentences, to the point, usually followed by the un-requested ZIP code.

MarlonDale had also begun collecting a variety of special items.

He collected all things shiny. He had shoe boxes filled with quartz rocks obtained on vacations or field trips. Each box had exactly a multiple of ten rocks and was labeled as such, including number of items and date of collection, with a black magic marker on the box end. "40-11/16/98".

MarlonDale's room was immaculate and orderly. An entire wall was covered with 10-foot long, white, 10-inch shelving. Each shelf displayed a variety of MarlonDale's collectibles. One entire shelf was lined with quartz rocks, recently obtained, not yet boxed. They were displayed in rows of five, at 45 degree angles, as if it were a striped parking lot for rocks. Another shelf contained plastic models of various airplanes, five rows, two deep, parked length-wise along the shelving as awaiting take-off on the 10-inch runway. There were military and civilian aircraft, alien spaceships, and several starship Enterprise versions.

Another shelf contained shiny aluminum collectibles, hubcaps, chrome auto detail strips, chromed lug nuts and chrome or aluminum inner tube valve extensions from his bicycle. These items were constantly rotated as MarlonDale stumbled across another hubcap or special shiny item while on his walks.

As a new object was added, the one on the farthest end of the shelf was removed, wrapped in today's paper (always the front page) to appropriately categorize the events of the day in which the item was retired.

MarlonDale's 'specials' were located in several, 5-foot high lawyers' bookcases next to his bed. These cases held his collection of electronics. The shelves contained radios, computers, calculators, telephones, portable TVs, a breadmaker and a crockpot, all in various stages of assembly and disassembly. MarlonDale had been using screwdrivers, wrenches and pliers since the age of 4 and was often busy taking appliances apart. Most of the time, they were discarded or otherwise replaced with a newer model and were free game.

His electronic collection was kept safely behind glass to avoid any dust or other particulate contamination. MarlonDale had wrapped the bookcases with aluminum foil to assure a consistent shininess with the glass front, and to protect the delicate transistors, capacitors and resistors from electromagnetic wave damage.

MarlonDale also loved sunflowers. The tall and spindly plants were a source of comfort since Terry first planted a few in the garden years earlier. MarlonDale was fascinated with them and often would watch them, or sit by them with his toys just to play near them. In a similar fascination, he loved water towers

Terry and Margherite would pull to the side of the road when passing a water tower so MarlonDale could take a picture or, if possible, get close enough to touch its supporting structure and pick up 10 rocks nearby.

MarlonDale's oddest compulsion was his absolute requirement to be outside at dusk to watch the street lamps come on.

Chapter 8

The pivotal Mercury Vapor Experience happened on a very cold January night. MarlonDale had spent the afternoon at Barnes and Noble leafing through reference books on Thomas Edison. His class had been studying inventors and MarlonDale was researching Thomas Edison.

Margherite had become a fixture at the B and N by then. Since the time MarlonDale and Layton were toddlers, the three of them frequented the first Barnes and Nobles in Chesterfield, as if it were a daycare for them and a therapy session for her. MarlonDale would read book jackets and on the way home recite, verbatim, everything he read, including reviews, author biography, ISBNs and publishers.

Margherite's depression and her ego required constant nurturing. The other housewives and patrons of the arts at B and N were willing to stroke her.

She read her works of positional poetry on Tuesday evenings to a small gaggle of her friends, taught Taoist quilting at the Thursday noontime craftworks, offered a biannual Renaissance art appreciation week in February, and joined a Friday morning book club.

MarlonDale occasionally brought in his latest collection of 10, whether it was quartz rocks, Dominoes, Mah Jong tiles or ten of the "Ctrl" keys he had removed from 10 keyboards. He would lay them out on a table, count, stack, re-arrange, recount.

The manager of the bookstore, Quinn Leruq, a gay middle-aged Frenchman, was empathetic to the needs and desires of artistic women. Quinn was happy to give Margherite and her sons room to run.

The hourly staff, on the other hand, was aggravated that these boys used the reference books, occasionally split bindings, and their mother rarely purchased anything except a scone or latte from Starbucks. However, hourly folks come and go, Quinn was a career employee at B and N and happy to please this representation of his mother's better side.

Chapter 9

Margherite and the boys had returned from the bookstore near dusk one evening. Marlon, of course, had to stay on the front porch awaiting the street lamps to light. It was in the low 20s, but he was wearing his shiny, silver parka. Layton had no quirks to speak of and went inside to watch television.

This was just before the millennium, November 1999. Terry had been in Washington, D.C., giving a presentation on "21st Century Virology, 22nd Century Logic," and was flying home on a red-eye at about 1 a.m.

Margherite stuck her head out of the front door after a few minutes, "MD, don't stay out anymore than 5 minutes after the lights come on, OK?"

"I think they are running slow tonight, see the flickering?" Marlon responded in his typical 10-word sentence structure.

"Hmm, I sure do. Well, 10 minutes then," and Margherite closed the door behind her.

"Ten minutes, I feel it may take 10^2 minutes tonight," MarlonDale spoke softly to himself.

The street lamps flickered to life within 20 minutes. Marlon watched and felt the usual satiety he had come to know when he witnessed the lights.

When asked to describe this first Mercury Vapor Experience, or MVE as it will be referred to hereinafter, Marlon at age 19, provided the following account.

"My first MVE happened when I was only a kid. I had read some scifi about trances, and altered states. So I didn't freak out or panic, anything like that. I was aware I was sitting on my front porch. But, I was also traveling, very fast, black hole speed. And I got there, where it was bright and shiny. Everything had a halogen luminescence that was warm and palpable. I didn't feel unusual or special in their, our world. I felt as comfortable there as at Barnes and Noble. "

At 1:15 a.m., Terry arrived home to find MarlonDale, lying on the snow-dusted porch, lips blue, skin ashen. Terry checked MarlonDale's carotid, and found a slow, weak pulse. His respirations were shallow at 8 per minute. MarlonDale was hypothermic and closing in on the Big Sleep. Terry unlocked the door, carried MD inside and started screaming for Margherite.

Margherite was asleep on the couch, the Discovery channel playing a story on how little the coming Millennium would affect the native tribes of New Guinea.

An empty martini shaker and glass, and half a bag of microwave popcorn told the story of Margherite's evening.

"Call 9-1-1, get me some blankets, dammit. Jesus, Margherite, how long has MD been out on the porch? He is freezing to death," Terry barked.

"Oh my God, I thought he came in and went to his room. He said he was only going to stay out 10 minutes," Margherite said, as she ran to their room to gather blankets and their wonderful down comforter she had gotten from Lands End.

Terry took MD's parka off, the crusted snow falling to the living room floor like flaky, dry skin. He wrapped him up in a blanket, and the down comforter.

"Go downstairs and get that space heater we used in the camper that one time. My God, what the hell were you thinking?" Terry continued to vocalize well over a comfortable decibel range.

Margherite pushed the thermostat up to 88 and went downstairs to get the heater. Layton woke up, took one look at his brother and started crying. Ashen and blue, wrapped in a white comforter, MarlonDale appeared as if all he were missing was the wooden box. Terry occupied Layton with a task and told him to gather more blankets from the bedrooms to warm up his brother.

The ambulance took 6 minutes to arrive. In that time, MarlonDale's color had improved and his heart rate had picked up a few beats per minute. He was moaning a bit.

The ER staff gradually warmed MarlonDale and the hospital kept him all day, monitoring his heart for abnormal rhythm.

He had regained full consciousness by 6 a.m. and was eating breakfast at 7. Terry spent the day shuttling between his lab for a meeting and MarlonDale's room. Margherite and Layton stayed in the room with MD.

MarlonDale had come close, another 30 minutes, and the chances for resuscitation would have been limited.

He seemed to suffer no ill effects from his first Mercury Vapor Experience. The Hendershat family left the hospital at 5 p.m.only to fight the rush hour traffic.

Chapter 10

Terry made the decision that evening for the family to obtain some professional help. The boys had gone to bed and he and Margherite were sitting on their living room couch separated by uncomfortable silence.

"Margherite, we have to do something. MarlonDale is clearly more than quirky. His collecting, the TenSpeak, the obsession with the street lights. And you, I am so pissed off. It is one thing to spend your days at a bookstore and your evenings writing or watching TV, but your behavior is becoming too eccentric. You're drinking way too much," Terry said.

"It was an accident, I am so sorry. You know I would never do anything to put the boys in harms way. I'll do better Terry, I'll try to be more normal from this day on. I swear," Margherite said.

"I don't think it is possible for you. You've been acting, becoming, well, honestly, more and more," Terry began. Margherite took advantage of the pause.

"Artists are always eccentric, Terry, you know that, that's why you love me, my weirdness, it balances your normality, we are yin/yang." Margherite coyly rationalized, knowing she had totally screwed up.

"Honey, I love you, but eccentric may not be the best descriptor. Eccentric is when old rich men pay strippers to clean their houses naked. Or if you started wearing Ann Taylor business suits during the day and Victoria's Secret at night, that would be eccentric behavior for you. And can I remind you that eccentric is only used to describe bizarre behavior by people of means. Poor people are just called crazy. Jesus Christ, two weeks ago, you were microwaving bag after bag of popcorn because you found a few popped kernels that had the appearance of poodle puppies. You still have a shoebox full of these popcorn puppies in the kitchen. I don't know if you are rubbing off on MarlonDale, or vice-versa," Terry swiped.

"You are really a piece of work, you know that?" Margherite snipped. "Don't put MarlonDale's quirkiness on me, mister. I suffered pain you will never know with his birth hoping to avoid this conversation. I was so worried, and so were you. It was your God damn dream, Terry, about his being special. So now he is. So there!" Margherite began to sob.

Terry moved closer to her on the couch and put his arm around her. He used his weight to make them both lean back into the bolsters.

"I'm sorry, you are right. I shouldn't have vented on you, despite the fact that you f'd up royally last night. I am worried, and scared too for MD, and you. I don't want the two of you to become some mother-son version of Howard Hughes," Terry said, hoping to gain some comedic relief from the tension.

"If I start saving my urine in mason jars, you can call the white suits and I will not complain. For now, I will try to be less involved within my artistic sense and more vigilant of the goings-on within the house. That doesn't necessarily solve the immediate issue. What do we do with MarlonDale?" Margherite asked.

"I've been asking myself the same question, too. And then rather unexpectedly, I thought of Mac Sutherland. I don't think you ever met her. In fact, I hadn't thought of her in years. We dated, way before you came into the picture. She was brilliant, uncannily perceptive. She knew she was going into psychiatry from day one. She went into psychiatry and specialized in adolescent behavioral disorders, Autism, ADD, ADHD and the like. I remembered reading in one of the alumni rags that she remained in Columbia for quite some time and was a full professor, and then moved, I think it was, to Belleville, Illinois, to open a practice. That was several years ago though. I'll see if I can find her. Maybe she could evaluate MarlonDale," Terry said.

Margherite was half listening, occupied with self chastisement. "What shall I do Terry? I feel awful. MarlonDale will blame me, like you did. Layton will probably figure he has to be his brother's protector, because their demented mother can't seem to even keep track of her own boys." Margherite sobbed, a few tears dripped onto Terry's shoulder.

"We'll work it out. Please be you, don't be anyone else. Just try to remain in the moment with the boys, and don't play with gasoline and matches, all right?" Terry squeezed Margherite and gave her a long kiss for assurance.

"How pretty was this doctor? Did you boink her in the cadaver lab or some other odd medical location?" Margherite smiled, remembering a few of their own meeting spots.

"No, nothing like that. Mac, that's McCalister Sutherland, was a gymnast and I put together this trapeze in my room hanging from the ceiling, and she would," Terry began.

"You are so full of shit." Margherite countered.

"You know me too well, my love. Missionary man, I am, I am," Terry sighed.

Chapter 11

Dr. McCalister Sutherland had traveled extensively conducting research and engaging in long discourses with European and Asian physicians studying what is now known as Pervasive Developmental Disorders. She had published well over 50 articles in peer reviewed journals. In other words, she knew her shit. Terry called the alumni office and tracked Dr. Sutherland to Belleville, Ill. He called her office and spoke briefly with her. Mac was glad to hear Terry was doing well as a researcher. She knew that was his calling. They discussed some good times. Mac broke the light chat. "So, Dr. Hendershat, why is it that you've called?"

Terry related his concern about MarlonDale. She listened as Terry provided a detailed history of Marlon's behavior since birth. She uttered a few "hmms" and "uh huhs" as he spoke. McCalister agreed to evaluate MarlonDale and they set up an appointment.

"Terry, I have been working with PDD kids and adults since the early '90s. We finally have a better understanding of the differences between the various disorders that have some similarities, including ADD, ADHD, ODD and OCD. I did several studies with NINDS, the National Institute for Neurological Disorders and Stroke, involving teens with Aspergers. It's really quite fascinating. Why don't you do some literature review before our visit? It may help you feel less isolated. These disorders are quite prevalent. You and, what did you say your wife's name was?" Dr. Sutherland asked.

"Margherite."

"Yes, Margherite. Reading some of the research may help you both feel less alone in this."

"I will certainly do that. Oh, and I didn't mention, but we have another son, 18 months younger than Marlon. But, Layton seems to be very normal, thank God," Terry said.

"Well, every family has to have one of them," Dr. Sutherland said.

"See you in a week, thanks again Mac. I am really looking forward to seeing you. It's really been too long," Terry said with a hint of remorse.

"Yes, it has, Dr. Hendershat, it has. See you soon, though," McCalister said.

Chapter 12

Terry relayed the news to Margherite over dinner. He explained to MarlonDale that they were going to visit an old friend of his from medical school who has been studying teenage behavior.

"I told her about your collections, and the TenSpeak. She was impressed and said that she had met a boy in Hong Kong with very similar habits. Dr. Sutherland is looking forward to meeting you. If you like, she may be able to get you in touch with the boy in Hong Kong to discuss things the two of you may have in common. Anyway, I told her about the street lamps and how we had the accident last week. I would like you to discuss that with her too if that is ok with you," Terry said.

"Do I get to go?" Layton asked.

"We are all going Layton. If you need to, or want to talk to her, I am sure we can arrange that," Margherite chimed in.

"It was just an accident, Mom fell asleep, that's all," Marlon said.

"It's not just that MD. We'd just like to understand you better and we think Dr. McCalister can help. Will you give it a try? She really is an interesting person and I know she will say the same about you."

"I will go and I will talk I will explain. I don't believe there is a Hong Kong kid, though. I think that is one way to get me in. But, I don't mind if you feel it is best."

"Thank you honey, I love you," Margherite said while she arranged her linguini into shapes resembling Napoleon's hat.

During the next few days, Terry did Internet research on Pubmed, Medline and the university's search engines. There was a plethora of articles and references on PDD.

Pervasive developmental disorders (PDD) refers to a group of behavioral disorders characterized by delays in the development of the child's socialization and communication skills. Parents usually note symptoms as early as infancy, although the typical age of onset is before 3 years of age. There are wide ranging degrees of symptomology, making the diagnosis difficult. Children may have difficulty in using and understanding language and often have difficulty relating to people. They may not respond to social cues in expected manners.

The child, adolescent or adult, may be unable to relate to objects or events occurring around them in a reasonable and appropriate fashion.

They may have difficulty with changes in routines or may be uncomfortable in new surroundings. Often times, they may exhibit repetitive body movements, speech patterns, or patterns of behavior similar to an obsessive compulsive disorder.

Autism is characterized by impaired social interaction, communication skills and limited interest in normal activity. It is thought to be due to a developmental brain disorder and is the most characteristic and best studied PDD. Other types of PDD include Asperger's Syndrome, Childhood Disintegrative Disorder, and Rett's Syndrome.

Terry thought the information was sufficiently vague that nearly any quirky kid could be diagnosed with a degree of PDD. But he intuitively knew MarlonDale was well outside the quirky ballpark. Had he known Margherite when she was a child, he surmised she would likely have been diagnosed with some form of PDD.

"The apple didn't fall too far from the maternal tree," Terry mumbled as he clicked through web pages.

Children with PDD vary widely in their abilities, intelligence, and behaviors. Some children do not speak at all, others speak in limited phrases or conversations, and some have relatively normal language development. There was nothing in the literature about TenSpeak. Terry figured that was MarlonDale's personal contribution to PDD.

Terry learned that children's playground activities usually included repetitive play skills with limited social interaction skills. Unusual responses to sensory information, such as loud noises and lights, or sudden unexpected movement, are very common.

PDD affects 4-5 of every 10,000 persons in some form. PDD is both a neurological and biological condition, with overlapping behavioral symptoms of unknown etiology. Sufficiently vague.

Chapter 13

Terry, Margherite, MarlonDale and Layton drove through the McDonalds for breakfast on their way to Dr. Sutherland's. MarlonDale had been eating Egg McMuffins and hash browns with coffee since Margherite took him there immediately after he gained his first tooth. The coffee was always half cream and lots of sugar. Margherite's passion for performance art and mantra quilting was only equaled by her love for fast food breakfasts, McDonalds usually, with Jack in the Box at a very close second.

They arrived at Dr. Sutherland's office and were surprised to find that the clinic was located within her residence. The not-quite-Victorian home was elegant and mysterious looking. Layton called it spooky.

"Dad, it's the house on Nickelodeon, the Munsters' house at 1313 Mockingbird Lane," Layton said.

"You're right, Layton. It does look a little like that," Margherite said. "I wonder if there is a furry Cousin IT scurrying around in there."

MarlonDale mentioned that he thought it looked interesting and hoped they could explore the house.

The three-story house looked to be every bit of 4,000 square feet. The first two stories were covered in clapboard siding, the third covered in shake shingles. The front porch was turret-like and extended the entire length of the home. Each level had a similar type porch, or outcropping, meticulously detailed in spindles and railings. There were three chimneys jutting out of the strongly-pitched roofs. Many of the upper level windows were round-topped, giving a church-like appearance. Smooth and brilliant white round copper guttering snaked around the eaves, reaching to the ground at all four corners.

The southeast end of the residence was apparently Dr. Sutherland's office. Four rectangular boards, 1" X 10" by 4 feet in length, hung from the uppermost porch eave.

"McCalister Sutherland, MD"
"Behavioral Psychiatry"
"Clinic and Research Facility"
"Hours by Appointment"

Terry parked the Volvo and the family stepped onto the porch. A welcome mat was embroidered with Dr. Sutherland's name, beckoning patients with large baroque letters, "Welcome Friends." The sign on the door said, "Please Come In."

Terry led the way into a massive hallway that was at least 12 feet wide. Both sides of the hallway were lined with Butternut Butler's pantries.

To the left of the entry way was an ornate roll top desk, occupied by a petite young woman, maybe 25, with a long brunette perm, wearing a light blue Nike Gortex running suit . She turned as they entered.

"Hi, I'm Emily, Dr. Sutherland's research assistant," she beamed with a smile and warmth. "And her aide, and secretary and nurse, butcher, baker and candlestick maker, to name just a few things I do. You must be Dr. Hendershat, Margherite, MarlonDale and Layton."

Handshakes went all around like the wave at a baseball game.

"Dr. Sutherland is finishing up with a patient. I need some forms filled out, as I am sure you know," Emily said.

Margherite bent over to her boys and whispered, "Well, she certainly doesn't look like Cousin IT, does she?" Layton giggled.

Emily handed Margherite and Terry sets of forms which they spent the next 20 minutes filling out, describing all things Hendershat, particularly MarlonDale Hendershat.

After a few more minutes, Dr. Sutherland came into the room through a heavy, oval, nine-foot door.

McCalister Sutherland was stunning, dressed in black. She had shoulder length platinum blonde hair, long silver hoop earrings, and a rope of silver pearls around her neck.

Terry immediately thought that she looked exactly as he remembered her, as if aging failed to reach her, still a size 6, he was certain.

She was wearing satin black bell bottom slacks, a black tightly-knitted V-neck top and a full-length black satin jacket with fringe along the sleeves. He recalled those elegant, sculpted cheekbones. Cheekbones that had the appearance of being ordered directly from the "Perfect Scandinavian Model Catalog" and were lightly painted with a sheen of silver pancake makeup.

MarlonDale thought, "She is so shiny, I am going to like her."

Chapter 14

Dr. Sutherland spoke first.

"Hello Terry, it has been such a long time. It is so nice to see you again," Dr. Sutherland said, extending her hand.

Terry took it and looked into her eyes,

"You look wonderful, Mac," Terry said.

A pregnant pause followed as Terry stared at her a little too long.

"This is my family, Margherite, Layton and MarlonDale," Terry said with a subtle uneasiness in his voice.

"Very nice to meet you, Dr. Sutherland," Margherite said, extending her hand.

"Please, do call me Mac, I wish you would, please?" Dr. Sutherland replied.

"You are wonderfully shiny and this house is very interesting," Marlon injected into the clumsy adult situation as his thumb and little finger tapped his thigh.

"Thank you, MarlonDale, it is a very old, interesting house. Perhaps after we get settled, you would like to explore. Let's take a look at some of the paperwork here. Can I leave you and Layton out here with Emily? I would like to talk to your mom and dad," Dr. Sutherland said as she looked at Emily.

Emily read Dr. Sutherland's suggestion and said, "Boys, how would you like to go upstairs to a really cool porch that overlooks the backyard? It's kind of high up, but you can see for miles, we might even be able to see a bald eagle flying around."

Dr. Sutherland took Terry and Margherite into her office. The room was entirely different than either of them expected. Instead of more heavy wood moulding and bulky valance and tapestry curtains, the room was light and airy. A corner contained a small garden, artificially lit with a growing light. It held mums, roses and amazingly, ten mature sunflowers, every bit of 5 feet high.

The original plank flooring had been sanded and clear-coated to a glossy sheen, reflective of the room. The leaded windows were all light-colored glass shapes which conducted a rainbow prism effect in the room. Wooden slat blinds were available in the event a patient required darkness.

A roll-top desk much like Emily's was wedged into the far corner opposite the garden.

Dr. Sutherland conducted business in the center of the room on a large Oriental rug of bright yellows, interspersed with tans, greens and maroons. Three overstuffed lawyers leather chairs and hassocks, an old-fashioned wooden scroll loveseat and a full-size couch crept inwards from the perimeter of the rug. Next to one of the chairs, obviously Dr. Sutherland's, was a tall lamp stand and end table. Dr. Sutherland's tape recorder and notepad lay on the table.

"Please, Margherite, Terry, both of you, here, have a seat," Dr. Sutherland said, pointing to the loveseat.

"This grand old house was built about 1891 or 1892. It was designed by a wonderfully interesting man, Henry Bacon. An architect, a devotee of the master Henry Hobson Richardson. Bacon rarely did private residences, this one is quite unusual. As you can tell, it has Victorian and Romanesque features. I didn't want to be stuck in a clinic atmosphere. I saw this place in a real estate magazine ad. I love the woodwork with its matching doors with transoms," Dr. Sutherland said.

"The pantries and closets are great places for record storage. Did you notice the large pocket doors along the hallway? Each side is made from a different wood for variety. Sets each room off from the rest of the house. Listen to me rattle off about this old place now. So, let us talk about MarlonDale and his behavior patterns," Dr. Sutherland said.

Terry spoke first.

"As I mentioned on the phone, MarlonDale was a normal delivery and was, and is, physically healthy. Our first indication was when Margherite noticed that he would not make eye contact. We thought maybe it was a cranial nerve dystrophy, but testing was negative for any organic pathology. He learned to walk by about 10 months, certainly unremarkable. Although to this day, he is rather awkward, clumsy, tripping or stumbling. He seems to have normal senses, but his response to stimuli is at times, inappropriate. But, he is a very loving boy whom I hope you can help," Terry said.

"Well, those are certainly PDD symptoms Terry, go on, please," Mac said.

Margherite picked up the conversation.

"He was using single words by 2 and phrases by 3. He learned to read early, too, and is a voracious reader," Margherite said. "He did have some unusual preoccupations as a toddler, playing with only one toy at a time, and he prefers shiny toys. He would only play one audible sound, a horse's whinny, on his barnyard play-and-speak. That was annoying." "But Dr. Sutherland, I'm sorry, Mac," Margherite continued, "What is rather peculiar is that, if you pay attention, he only speaks in 10-word sentences.

It is bizarre how he manages a conversation automatically with 10 words. We have come to call it MarlonDale's Tenspeak. His teachers accept it and he does well in school. But it is strange, don't you think?"

"Honestly, it's not necessarily unusual within the context of PDD," Dr. Sutherland said. "There are several possibilities that come to mind, several disorders. Terry, I am sure you researched a few of them. I am leaning towards Asperger's as a primary potential diagnosis. We can do some testing, and of course, some talking I am sure MarlonDale will have a lot to say. Even though it will come out in short sentences."

"Do you want to talk to all of us first, or MarlonDale alone? How do you want to do this?" Terry asked.

"I would like to talk to MarlonDale alone this visit. We'll certainly have family sessions down the road. I'd love to start today, unless you don't have time."

"Let's get started today, now," Margherite said, with quick, clipped words, as if hurrying would help.

"I am sure Terry mentioned my screw-up the other night when MarlonDale almost froze to death on the porch due to his incessant street lamp watching. And my inattention, I have to admit," Margherite said.

Dr. Sutherland straightened up in her chair.

"Terry mentioned that there was an incident of some kind. But he didn't elaborate, perhaps you want to expound?"

Margherite explained the drama of the night in question, along with a few interspersed, mitigating factors. Dr. Sutherland nodded her head and thanked her for sharing the difficult story. She took out her Blackberry and sent a text message to Emily telling her to return the boys to the clinic.

Terry and Margherite explained to Layton and MarlonDale that today was MarlonDale's day to talk, and Layton's would be another day. Emily took the Hendershat family for a walk around the grounds while MarlonDale and Dr. Sutherland talked.

Chapter 15

   MarlonDale shook hands with Dr. Sutherland
again. She directed him to one of the overstuffed
chairs. MarlonDale was immediately detoured to
the sunflowers. He stood in front of them,
cocked his head to the side like a dog hearing a
silent whistle. He stared at them and Dr.
Sutherland made a note that he appeared to be
listening to them. Dr. Sutherland watched him
for about a minute and then asked MarlonDale
what it was he liked about the sunflowers.

   "I especially like their shape, thin stem, large
round top," MarlonDale replied.

   "I like sunflowers, too, that's why I grow
them yearly. Do you like other things as much as
the sunflowers?" Dr. Sutherland asked.

   "I like water towers and street lamps just the
same," Marlon indicated.

   "How do you feel when you are near those
things?"

   "Safe and comfortable while I am near or
under them," MarlonDale answered.

   "Has anything special ever happened to you
while watching them?" Dr. Sutherland asked.

   MarlonDale had never fully explained his
fascination with sunflowers, water towers and
street lamps to anyone. He always felt that it was
his secret and that he could not share with
anyone, not Layton or his friends at school.

Today, for the first time in his life, he felt a calm settle upon him as he sat in this house with this shiny woman. MarlonDale looked at Dr. Sutherland, this time directly in her eyes. Dr. Sutherland met his gaze.

She was the first human being MarlonDale ever told about the Mercury Vapor Experience. He was particularly detailed in his explanation, its content and tone well ahead of a 10-year-old's ability. His narration was received by Dr. Sutherland in common kings English, TenSpeak was not required.

He delivered the story without uttering a sound.

Chapter 16

MarlonDale telepathically downloaded his entire life's events folder to Dr. Sutherland. His birth, infancy, toddlerhood and everything he had experienced to this point. Sent effortlessly, nearly instantaneously in silence.

"I have had this secret for as long as I can remember. That I am more than just special, that I have a particular purpose for being special, that I have a destiny to fulfill awaiting me. It started with the sunflowers my dad grew. When they reached 6 feet, I would go near them and they would communicate with me in the breeze. Nothing I could understand or define, just a feeling of connectedness. The same thing happened with water towers and street lamps. I would throw a tantrum if we were driving somewhere and passed a water tower. As we would come within a mile or so, I would feel the tower pulling me. I always gave Dad or Mom advanced notice to slow down. They were usually cooperative and pulled over, unless we were in a hurry, like Mom had some recital or something," MarlonDale said.

"When I was little, they would walk me up as close to the tower as possible and I would look up until they shook me and told me we had to leave. As I got bigger they stayed in the car. If I was able to actually touch, or even better, climb up on the water tower, the wispy communication became palpable. My skin would bristle and I would feel warm, hot even. It wasn't as if the towers talked to me, or told me to do anything, but I felt a kind of bond. No, more like a dependence, or interdependence, an, alliance, yes, that's the best word to describe it, an alliance with water towers. Like we were in it together, whatever it is," MarlonDale continued.

"I felt a similar connection to street lights, but because they are so prevalent, I didn't have the compulsion or the need to meld with them. They were always around. But then it happened. I had a Mercury Vapor Experience and everything became apparent with a crystalline lucidity. I paged through Dad's Thesaurus looking for the right word to describe how clearly I understand, and crystalline lucidity works for me."

Dr. Sutherland smiled and sent an affectionate confirmation to MarlonDale.

"I would love to hear more about your MVE Marlon," Dr. Sutherland said.

Chapter 17

"I feel you know what I am going to say. Do I really have to explain it all to you?" MarlonDale said out loud, breaking the silence and reverting to TenSpeak. He was not a favorite of idle chatter when the point had already been made.

Dr. Sutherland answered in kind, "Please, MarlonDale, there's a reason that you must tell me. I can explain after you have told me your story. There are many things you know, but many you don't."

Returning to his nonTenSpeak telepathy, MarlonDale continued his saga.

"I really was not sure why I had this fascination with street lights until last week. We're studying great inventors in Mrs. Tellender's class. I was assigned Thomas Edison. Mom took us to Barnes and Noble for her poetry night, and I took the opportunity to use the biography section to read up on Mr. Edison. I found out that he may have been like me. The bio said that he was thought to be 'addled,' which I figured back then probably meant he was not right.

That's what they say about me all the time. I'm not right. Anyway, he was raised a lot by his mom too, like me. When he was a boy, he invented his own language and taught it to his brothers and sisters, kind of like a code, like me with my TenSpeak. He was a collector, too, and had collections of all kinds of things as a boy and as a man. I wrote this down. Hold on."

MarlonDale took a pocket notebook from his jacket pocket and opened up the spiral pad. He always kept a pad handy. MarlonDale read without uttering a sound, "*Edison's lab contained a collection of odds and ends. Eight thousand kinds of chemicals.*

Every kind of screw made, every size of needle, every kind of cord or wire, hair of humans, horses, cows, rabbits, goats, minx, camels, silk in every texture, cocoons, various kinds of hoofs, sharks teeth, deer horns, tortoise shells, corks, resin, varnish and oil, ostrich feathers, peacocks tail, jet, amber, rubber, all ores and a magnificent collection of quartz stones, categorized by date and location of collection."

"Dr. Sutherland," MarlonDale continued, "I do that. I have boxes of quartz rocks. It's really weird reading about someone born 150 years ago being like me, don't you think?" MarlonDale asked just as an inquisitive boy would. "And Dr. Sutherland, I wrote this quote of his down, *'To invent, you need a good imagination and a pile of junk.* And you should see my room, I have a lot of stuff everyone else calls junk. So, am I going to be like Edison, an inventor or something like that?" There was excitement in his thoughts.

Dr. Sutherland responded as they continued their muted conversation, "There are many things that you will learn about yourself, your past, as well as your future. You are here for a reason, dear MarlonDale, and I will be your guide, so to speak, to help you reach your potential."

MarlonDale heard her fail to answer his question. He continued.

"He used shiny tin foil to make the first phonograph recording, did you know that? And he really liked shiny stuff, too. Most of his filaments and chemical processes involved silver or tungsten or mercury, which have a flicker, and glow. I like shiny, because it comes back," MarlonDale said as his head took a cocked stance and upward gleam. "Stare at something black, you get nothing in return for your time. Look at something shiny, it looks back, it is involved in you, it listens."

MarlonDale's head returned to center and he continued, "Edison designed a fluoroscope which worked like x-rays and he also made the first motion picture camera. It's the fact that he harnessed light for power, such as seeing through bodies, and used light to display another reality by developing movies. And so I put this all together that night on the porch when the street lamps came on and bingo. I got it."

"What is it that you got, MarlonDale?" Dr. Sutherland asked.

MarlonDale's face expressed a tired ennui of frustration. "Do I have to think everything to you, can't you just skip ahead in my mind?" MarlonDale asked.

"Yes, you have to tell me the whole story and no, I won't just skip to the end. Please, MarlonDale, go on," Dr. Sutherland said as she leaned forward, placing her chin on steepled fingers.

"I figured it out when I saw them after the lights came on that night. You see, Edison's Mercury Vapor light could be used for illuminating not only the dark, but also creating a new reality, like a movie or an x-ray, like what he worked on in the early days at Menlo Park. I spent a few lunch hours at our school's library looking up the history of street lighting. When Mom did Renaissance Posture and Poetry

Appreciation week, I used the Barnes and Nobles reference shelves. Early on, they used candles with these special metal filament wicks, in metal boxes to light the streets of Philadelphia. My guess is that these filaments emanated something similar to the Mercury Vapor lights. Because our civilization was not advanced enough to develop electricity yet, these crude candles did the trick. Benjamin Franklin was the first to mandate that the street be lit in the evening. He was an inventor too and my guess is that he was along the same line as Edison, another one of them. Or rather, Edison was like Franklin, I guess I should say. Did you know that Ben Franklin was the postmaster there in Philadelphia? I don't think the street lights were for nighttime mail delivery, do you?" MarlonDale asked.

He was able to get a diminutive smile from Dr. Sutherland, expanding her extraordinary cheekbones.

MarlonDale continued, "Franklin knew what was going on with the night and the lights, he knew, even way back then. And then Edison came along. After Thomas Edison developed light bulbs, he made some especially for street lamps using a different type of filament which used mercury excited by an electric charge to make light. The reaction took place in a small quartz tube that was inside a larger bulb that was made of silicon, all shiny materials, I might add. The older tubes put out a bluish-green light that was bright enough, but it made people look pale and sick, like their blood was drained from them, almost like they were under a fluoroscope. You get it Dr. Sutherland, you know," Dr. Sutherland's head nodded ever so slightly.

"It's these special filaments that put the 'others' into a trance or whatever so they don't experience the existence of this unusual reality. Those early lights also put out ultraviolet light, too. If you stared at them too long, your eyes would become inflamed. So, some 20 years ago, they started putting filters on them, an extra outer bulb which kept the UV light from getting out. And they put an extra safety precaution of a strip of carbon on the lamp's electrode which would burn the light out if the bulb filter cracked. Maybe that is what happened the other night when they came out. They had to come and fix the light.

But this different reality that the street lights offered up, the one with ET's, remained unseen by most people. For some reason, that night, I saw them, and this new world of activity became tangible to me. And so every night, I know something is going on, something really strange and fascinating, something I have to witness. I read that sometime in the next 10 years, no one will be able to install new mercury vapor lamps. So sometime in the next ten years everything will change. Well, everything for other people will change, it has already changed for me, and I guess you, too."

"MarlonDale, that was a very interesting and coherent narrative. You mentioned 'they' came out, MarlonDale, who are they?" Dr.Sutherland asked.

"I call them the repairmen, but you and I both know who they are." Marlon smirked and slid his thumb and forefinger across his lips in the 'my lips are sealed' motion.

"I watched them when they came that night on the porch. The street light was dying and it was cycling. When the bulbs get older, they need more and more voltage to maintain the arc discharge, which raises the pressure in the tube. It eventually gets so high that the voltage exceeds the voltage of the ballast switch and the light goes out. But then, because the light went out, the pressure drops and the ballast fires up the lamp again, so it goes on, and then off and then on. It's like it knows it is dying, but it wants to live so it keeps trying. The repairmen, I think, are kind of like paramedics for lights. They come out and try to save the light, shock it a few times and if it works, they go away. If not, they take the light down and replace it with a new one.

The new ones are really advanced. A bunch of companies have gotten into the street lamp business, GE, Westinghouse, American Electric, Thomas and Betts and the Line Material Company. They have so many different models and versions. One of the newest is called the Silverliner. I can tell when a Silverliner is up, cause the reality switching, the street roll up is a lot quicker."

Dr. Sutherland leaned back in her chair and crossed her legs. She scribbled a few notes, her silver hoop earrings swaying as she changed positions. Telepathically, Marlon heard her say, "Marlon, tell me what happens next. I want you to be very specific as to what it is you experience."

"Ok. It's not exactly the same every time. But there are some consistent factors. At the moment the street lights flicker, the sky changes. Billowy clouds become stringy and effervescent. The sky becomes grey, and looks like a bowl of boiling grits. Bubbly and angry. The air changes and becomes heavy. Waves form all around, and you see everything as if through spaces between Venetian blinds. And time, time does not register once the Mercury Vapor Lamps begin flickering. The flickering leads to the continuous emission of a vaporous light from the friendly Silverliner.

The light, like a steady rain, bathes you and everything it touches. It's like swimming, totally in the medium. The surrounding envelope around you is a comfortable steady 80 degrees. I know, because I've measured it any number of times with a digital thermometer I keep on the porch. It's a parallel, evening universe theatre without having to buy a ticket. And only I can see the show."

Dr. Sutherland folded her notepad and laid it gently on the table. She stood and clasped her hands together. They made a subdued clap.

"MarlonDale, unfortunately our hour has about come to an end," Dr. Sutherland said in vocalized TenSpeak. "We will continue this conversation next week, regularity is important. And we must keep secret our silent communication ability, yes?"

Her voice was steady and did not have any indication that she was in any way surprised by what he had told her.

"Dr. Sutherland, everyone but you already thinks I'm way wierd. Say anything about telepathic communication with my new doctor, right. Dad would call the nut squad for both of us," MarlonDale said.

She smiled. Dr. Sutherland text messaged Emily to bring the Hendershats back to the office.

Chapter 18

Dr. Sutherland had not performed a physical examination of any kind, had not probed MarlonDale's psyche or used any of the hundred of psychological profile testing protocols available to evaluate behavior disorders. Nevertheless, she had come to a conclusion and sat Terry and Margherite in the overstuffed leather chairs to discuss MarlonDale's disorder

"MarlonDale is a delightful boy, communicative, receptive to interaction. He certainly does have a distinct avoidance for eye contact. The TenSpeak is quite remarkable, done without any apparent effort. He did display a couple different ritualistic patterns of behavior. The finger-to-thigh tapping you mentioned to me, Terry, motor tics, all very common and may be transient. Have you noticed MarlonDale uses a ritualistic repetitive breathing pattern?" she asked.

"No, I am not quite sure what you mean, Mac?" Terry said.

"I noticed he inspires five relatively easy, normal, lung volumes. They are followed by two deep inhalations and deep exhalations. Then, three of the normal volumes, it's TenSpeak Breathing. Watch him on the way home and count it out," Dr. Sutherland said.

"I guess it is no more unusual than any of his other quirkiness," Margherite indicated.

"I believe that MarlonDale has a variant of Aspergers Disorder. Terry, are you familiar with Aspergers, did you research it?" Mac asked Terry, doctor to doctor, former lover to lover, leaving Margherite out of the conversation.

Terry told Mac, moreso for Margherite's benefit, what he had found about Aspergers.

"I researched Aspergers Disorder in the DSM IV for the diagnostic criteria. I made up, basically, a scorecard for Marlon's behavior. Let me read this and you can tell me what you think," Terry said.

Terry took out a spiral notepad the size of a day planner from his pocket. Like son, like father. He described the characteristics of Aspergers, some factors that MarlonDale exhibited, and discounted others that MarlonDale did not display.

For the benefit of Margherite, and to help Dr. Sutherland, he described the condition and how each factor related to his son.

"Aspergers is characterized by:

    A. *A qualitative impairment in social interaction, as manifested by at least two of the following*:

    (1) *Marked impairment in the use of multiple nonverbal behaviors such as eye-to-eye gaze, facial expression, body postures, and gestures to regulate social interaction.*

MD has not made eye-to-eye contact since he was little, and he frequently rocks in chairs and couches, he makes inappropriate faces all the time and now we find his breathing pattern is ritualistic. That's one for Aspergers.

(2) Failure to develop peer relationships appropriate to developmental level.
Marlon has some friends at school and some who he meets at the library, primarily the result of Margherite's socializing with their parents, so I am equivocal on this one.

(3) A lack of spontaneous seeking to share enjoyment, interests, or achievements with other people. Well, MarlonDale does not really share a lot with me, or Margherite, but he does seem to share his time with Layton, and does seem to enjoy a select few friends. He will share items that are not his, such as the books at Barnes and Noble, or drawings he made with their crayons on their paper. But he will not let anyone disturb any of his collections. Another one for Aspergers.

(4) Lack of social or emotional reciprocity. Yea, well, I have to call this number three for Aspergers. Marlon definitely does not respond in kind. He does not hug back or respond with a return 'I love you.' The best we can get is, 'Yea mom, yea dad.' It was difficult in the beginning.

(5) *Restricted repetitive and stereotyped patterns of behavior, interests, and activities. Encompassing preoccupation with one or more stereotyped and restricted patterns of interest that is abnormal either in intensity or focus.* Marlon scores high here. His fascination with street lamps, water towers, outer space, decimals, TenSpeak, his collection of quartz crystals and rocks that have quartz in them. He must have a dozen shoe boxes filled with quartz, labeled as to date and location of collection

Margherite interjected, "Remember when he was in first grade and they had a lecture on household safety and things like poisons under the sink, and they gave those green Mr. Uck stickers with that frowning face. MarlonDale came home with a few stickers and put them on everything in the refrigerator. He became obsessed that everything in the kitchen that we ate or drank could be poison. He was deeply suspicious about everything and we would have to taste his food first before he ate it. It went on for every bit of six months and he just grew out of the idea that everything was poison."

Terry continued, "MarlonDale's focus can be every bit as intense as a PhD candidate. He studies and learns, has an incredible vocabulary, it is a fascinating fascination, I just wish it wasn't my kid that was so fascinatingly unusual."

(6) *Apparently inflexible adherence to specific, nonfunctional routines or rituals.*

Marlon rings the bell here too. He has to be outside or at least at a window at dusk to catch the street lights come on, hell or high water.

He has an almost ceremonial routine for matters of hygiene. He loves being totally immersed in water and can swim quite well, but washing face and hands requires an entire sequence of events such as walking in the bathroom backwards for reasons he does not explain. The temperature of the water has to be exact, 105 degrees, two squirts of liquid anti-bacterial soap per hand. I don't want to elaborate, but there are many dysfunctional routines in our household that we have come to accept. We put in an extra bathroom just for MarlonDale so Layton wouldn't be late for school.

(7) *Stereotyped and repetitive mannerisms.* Marlon is always tapping his thigh with his thumb to fifth digit, both hands simultaneously, each hand, five taps, total of 10 taps, the decimal fixation. The

rocking back and forth is also done 10 times, brief pause, and then he resumes. And now we realize he even breathes in pattern. Score another for the Aspergers diagnosis.

(8) *Persistent preoccupation with parts of objects.* Marlon has been taking things apart for quite some time. He took apart his speak and spell, his baby monitor and then moved up to radios, coffee makers, cable boxes. The parts would be laid out neatly, classified by type of material and size of item.

(9) *The disturbance causes clinically significant impairment in social, occupational, or other important areas of functioning.* MarlonDale is impaired, but not necessarily to a significant degree. I am ambivalent about this one. Marlon is engaged socially at school, the library, and has occasionally spent the night at JoHanna Ann's house, a friend from school. I think we should pass on crediting him fully with this characteristic.

(10) *There is no clinically significant delay in language.* Marlon was speaking single words early and was communicative.

(11) *There is no clinically significant delay in cognitive development or in the development of age-appropriate self-help skills, adaptive behavior (other than in social interaction), and curiosity about the environment in childhood.* Clearly true about Marlon.

(12) *Criteria are not met for another Pervasive Developmental Disorder or Schizophrenia.* He's not schizophrenic and he seems to meet many of the Aspergers characteristics. I wonder if anyone in my family, or Margherite's may have a genetic predisposition," Terry considered.

Dr. Sutherland prepped to respond to Terry's concerns. She swept her hair behind her ears, crossed her legs and clasped her fingers over one knee.

"Terry, Margherite, Aspergers is a relatively new behavioral diagnostic entity. The genetic relevancy factor has yet to be fully explored. The exact etiology of the disorder, even neurobiologically, is unknown. I can give you a historical context if you like," Dr. Sutherland said.

Margherite nodded her head and leaned forward.

"Yes, please, Mac," Margherite said. "I would like to know as much as I can. You physicians are able to intellectualize these things with facts and statistics. I need to know how and why MarlonDale is the way he is, and why Layton isn't, and if there is something I did in the pregnancy or something in my genes, whatever."

"Of course Margherite, I will tell you what I know," Dr. Sutherland said.

Chapter 19

Dr. Sutherland offered the couple an explanation of the historical aspects of Autism and Aspergers disorder.

She explained that Aspergers is commonly listed under a general heading of "Pervasive Developmental Disorders." And that most of her colleagues believe it is a mild form of Autism, however, she also advised that these same 'colleagues' believed that Vioxx was a good pain medication until people started dropping dead from heart attacks and strokes.

She explained that research on Autism indicated there may be a genetic component, but it is not believed to be a single genetic flaw, but a combination of genes that create a vulnerability or a predisposition to Autism. It seemed to favor males, nearly five to one.

Margherite leaned forwards, elbows on her knees staring at Mac as she continued. Dr. Sutherland advised that in some cases, despite the genetic combination suggesting the potential for Autism, the social environment and cultural influences on the child render the gene flow as irrelevant as a lead bullet for a werewolf.

Terry and Margherite were relieved to hear that the outcome for Aspergers is often positive, adults can go to college or work productive jobs. The social and communication deficits are less severe in Aspergers than Autism.

She told them that because Aspies are able to communicate, they typically are placed in a normal social, school environment. This can be helpful to the developmental process, but may also be traumatic. Asperger's kids often are the object of criticism, taunts and teases by schoolmates who find the Aspergers behavior too strange to be ignored or accepted, making them easy targets for bullies. Aspies may respond to their classmate's cruelty by withdrawing to a self-imposed isolation, or in the opposite, may demonstrate increased abnormal behavior. The teases and taunts act as accelerants to their unusual quirks. "Has MarlonDale complained of being bullied, taunted or teased excessively?" Mac asked.

"No. Not at all," Margherite answered. "He seems to get along well at school."

"I'm glad to hear that, it makes life much easier." Dr. Sutherland said. She continued her lecture on Aspergers and told them that even though the quirky circumscribed interests are more prominent in Aspergers, their verbal IQ is usually higher than Autistics.

She mentioned that a pathognomonic feature of Aspergers is their clumsiness, thought to be due to an abnormal development of their proprioceptive abilities in maintaining a normal kinesthetic sense.

"They seem to have difficulty with position sense and location. Position of their body in relation to the external world. They may see the six or seven porch steps ahead. But their brain is unable to time the stepping up. It often results in frequent falls, missteps, trips and bruises."

Margherite nodded vigorously. "MarlonDale is a bit clumsy for sure. But his friend, JoHanna Ann is a real klutz. I wonder if she has Aspergers."

"Or maybe she is just a clumsy child Margherite. Let's focus on MD," Terry said.

Dr. Sutherland ignored their small tiff and explained that a family history correlation is being studied and indicates a high degree of positivity.

"I have to wonder Margherite," Terry began, "whether it is coincidental that your passion and lifelong study has involved proprioception and Renaissance artists that use body position sense in classical works of art."

"I knew it would end up my fault," Margherite took a handkerchief from her purse and blew her nose.

"I'm sorry honey," Terry said. It's a bit much that's all."

Dr. Sutherland continued on. "Aspergers disorder was identified by a Viennese psychiatrist, Hans Asperger. One early text cited an interesting speech pattern he exhibited. Dr. Asperger spoke only in short, concise and coherent sentences. His speech was always a tapestry of short, crisp sentences. Perhaps our good Dr. Hans Asperger spoke in Ten Speak?'

Terry shook his head slowly, absorbing the information.

Dr. Sutherland told Margherite and Terry that other researchers have postulated that when an ADHD co-exists with an Aspergers disorder, the frustration the Aspie feels in his inability to respond to the normal social environment will often lead to violence. She told them medication had been used effectively with patients who would take a baseball bat to a TV, stuff hamsters into Hobart dough makers, or push bullies down a flight of steps. The medicative effect is one similar to partial lobotomy.

"You should know, I am not a proponent of medication."

Chapter 20

"Well, Mac, what do we do? We've provided a loving home for MarlonDale. I don't know what else we could have done to," Terry said, as Margherite interrupted.

"Yes, we have a nuclear family," Margherite said defensively. "I admit, I am a bit, uh zealous and, um, idiosyncratic in my work, but I am always there as a mother."

Terry looked over at his wife and breathed out a deep sigh of something, just south of aggravation.

"Margherite, I was going to say, before you interrupted, that I can't imagine what more of a nurturing experience we could have provided for MarlonDale," Terry said. "We have accepted, and in some cases, encouraged his obsessive behaviors: the rock collecting, the hygiene, the stopping at water towers and the street lamp situation.

Are we enabling him to the point he will not be able to view the world in any other way, except through his own perception? Are we furthering his weirdness?"

Dr. Sutherland offered a nod and smile to both parents.

"Your very loving and tolerant home has helped MarlonDale. He is a special boy, with talents yet to develop. I would not recommend any change in the 'home' atmosphere," Dr.

Sutherland said, emphasizing the word "home." "I have several patients with Aspergers in phases of treatment. We've experienced remarkable successes, depending on the patient's commitment level. Terry, it is much like treatment for Tuberculosis, without medication."

Margherite looked puzzled but before she could speak, Terry explained.

"Honey, TB deeply infects the patient's lungs," Terry said. "The treatment requires that the patient take 2 or more medications, on a regularly scheduled basis for months and sometimes, depending on the extent of the infection, for years. The mycobacterium is very difficult to completely kill unless the patient is committed to following the treatment regimen. Miss a few doses, and the bacteria can gain strength and infect a broader area of pulmonary tissue, making it even more difficult to stop when treatment is resumed."

Margherite nodded, hoping the two of them would speak less medical-ese.

Dr. Sutherland stood, taking a step towards Terry and Margherite.

"Our special type of counseling takes the place of medication. I'd like to start a consistent integrative counseling session program," Dr. Sutherland said. "We start with ten, weekly, one-on-one dialogue sessions. Each session will be a minimum of 2 hours long. MarlonDale and I, we will learn much about each other. He'll gain a viewpoint and appreciation of my world, life. That's the reason we work here out of my home. We use standard functional, IQ, behavioral, empathic and insight testing. His test scores should significantly improve by the tenth session. I will be in contact with his teachers at school. The second phase includes ten weekly sessions of group therapy. These sessions are on weekends, five hours in length. We engage them in patient-to-patient interaction and planning. They actually begin to function as a cohesive team unit. They develop goals and objectives that are specific for them. I would say it is akin to military boot camp. Each one coming in with their own interests and abilities. These are turned inside out, exchanged for a new vision. A vision that uniquely comprehends the other, overall, encompassing reality. They will gain an ability to feel and respond appropriately. The end result, a reprogramming of neural pathways towards normal. It may take 100 sessions, it may take a thousand. The only way to know is to begin the process."

Terry looked over the side cushion of his chair at Margherite. She was wiping a tear from her left eye. During the last few minutes of Dr. Sutherland's recommendation, Margherite had removed a silk, leopard-spotted boa scarf, from her purse. She delicately wrapped the scarf over her head, around her neck twice, almost like a Berka, putting an arm's length of it behind her.

She then wrapped her right wrist twice with the scarf remaining in front. Terry wondered if she was planning on davening next. He also wondered whether he should sign Margherite up for some counseling with Dr. Sutherland. Perhaps he could get a discount.

"What do you think Margherite? Would you like to discuss this at home?" Terry asked.

"Dr. Sutherland, do you think it possible that MarlonDale may be able to understand that his obsession with water towers and street lamps is irrational behavior?" she asked.

"My hope is that he realizes you think it irrational," Dr. Sutherland said. "He will likely continue to collect, obsess and thigh tap. But, with an appreciation of how others view this behavior. In time, he may develop more culturally, socially, acceptable obsessions."

Margherite replied, "Then I can think of no reason we should not use this therapy. Do you, Terry?"

"No, I suppose not," Terry said. "Mac, should we consider any medications? We have tried a few over the years, but nothing seems to be effective in doing anything more than providing a sedative-type effect."

Margherite added, "Remember when he was little, I took him to my chiropractor, Dr. Lazarus? MarlonDale did improve with adjustments and the acupuncture. His thigh tapping and head rolling almost completely stopped. He had prescribed some nutritional supplementation including Omega-3 fatty acids and high doses of B vitamins. Should we consider something like that, too?"

Terry answered.

"Yes, and then he recommended Chelation therapy and although I like Dr. Lazarus, I could not find anything in the literature to support Chelation. So, we stopped the care. Maybe that was a mistake," Terry said.

"Terry, I understand your paradigm as an infectious disease specialist. For all of what you do, medications are key components," Mac said. "In Marlon's case, drugs and sedation are not my recommendations. I believe MarlonDale's brain 'chemistry' is as good as mine. CAM, complementary and alternative medicine are often used with Autism. True, there aren't a lot of well, scientifically-designed studies. But, dietary considerations, perhaps spinal alignment and nutrients, may help. You may certainly contact Dr. Lazarus if you so desire.

We are just going to establish more normal, neuronal connections. He may experience somnolence or euphoria with the weekly sessions. He may not respond to the sessions with any emotion. However, each week is re-writing the map of his brain. I will prescribe meds only if we absolutely have to," she took a step towards the door to her office.

"Emily will schedule the next ten-visit block of therapy," Dr. Sutherland continued. "I prefer you drop him off and pick him up. He needs an entire hour encompassed completely in my world. Oh, one other particularly important detail you must agree to. This reprocessing, reinventing, reconstructing of neuronal territory remains our secret. And by our, I mean only mine and his, MarlonDale's. I can share the results of the journey for sure. No details of the process other than what I've said. I hope you understand and trust that this is best."

"I suppose that will be alright," Margherite paused, gingerly wiping another tear away with the silky phylacteries. "Terry, if you and Dr. Sutherland, sorry, Mac, have confidence that this is really the best approach, that is enough for me. I can't say I completely understand, but,"

Terry looked Mac directly in her perfectly round, crisp azure eyes, trying to read her, like he had done while they were in med school. He was searching for a signal of comfort that everything was going to be alright, that he could lay his head on her chest, listen to the radio playing the new Boston release, and sleep. Mac was perfectly compliant and satisfied him with a lengthy, warm gaze.

With a hand on Terry and Margherite's shoulder, Mac said softly, "Trust me, MarlonDale will surely develop into a splendid human. He will express love, hope, trust and assuredly influence others."

Chapter 21

Emily scheduled MarlonDale for weekly visits with Dr. Sutherland. The visits continued for the next seven years. The session frequency varied from daily to weekly, to bimonthly, depending on the need, as expressed by Dr. Sutherland.

Despite the mystery of the process in the counseling sessions, the Hendershats were pleased with MarlonDale's progress.

As he entered his teenage years, his eccentricities lessened. He collected and cateogrized shiny items of 10 less often and became very interested in the cosmos. He spent more time with telescopes and at the planetarium than with quartz rocks and water towers. He still maintained the street light vigil every evening, but came into the house within five minutes of the lighting.

MarlonDale was clearly exhibiting more empathic behavior. At dinner one night, he announced how strange his TenSpeak must seem to them. He told them how he had tried several times to speak in a normal manner and found it impossible.

This was the first time he had ever discussed this quirk and how it must be perceived by others, a breakthrough according to Margherite. Dr. Sutherland told them to expect similar bursts of resonance as different axons and dendrites in Marlon's brain connect.

During several of the middle school parent-teacher conferences, MarlonDale's teachers indicated how well he seemed to have adapted. He displayed a developing social conscience for himself and others. Several of the school administration personnel who had known MarlonDale, since elementary school, said the change was quite remarkable. They asked what attributed to the change.

Terry and Margherite were more than happy to identify Dr. Sutherland's clinic, but due to the secrecy concerning the process, were unable to relate what led to the change.

Chapter 22

By the tenth grade, MarlonDale had become part of a small group of friends. They met in the morning before school at a local 'Jack in the Box' over coffee. At least three nights per week, they met at Barnes and Noble, where Mr. Leruq welcomed them as openly as he had welcomed Margherite.

On occasion, they were witness to Margherite's readings and enthusiastically applauded. Elevated levels of caffeine and a variety of brain disorders contributed to their appreciation of MarlonDale's mom screaming obscenities in contorted positions in front of a four-foot–by-four-foot canvas covered with burlap coffee sacks and strips of shag carpeting with her version of the Last Supper painted over the rough surfaces.

Each of his friends had their own oddities, a mixture of Attention Deficit Disorders, anxiety disorders, eating disorders, and bipolar disorders. His best friend, JoHanna Ann, had been diagnosed with ADHD and took a variety of medications to stay focused. She was unable to drive, relying on a willing and increasingly self-actualized, socially conscious MarlonDale for transportation.

MarlonDale had obtained his driver's license and was ecstatic with his mobility. The freedom of wheels was unlike any other aspect of his life to that point.

On the first day in which he drove himself to Dr. Sutherland's clinic, she was equally thrilled and told him, "The autonomous liberation you feel today is but a fraction. Your destiny includes an autarchy you cannot imagine right now. My son, you will quickly grow into your inescapable destiny."

MarlonDale just felt that it was cool to drive.

Chapter 23

The first few years of counseling, before
MarlonDale could drive, were re-run trips for
Margherite. Margherite would pull into the
drive in front of the old home. MarlonDale
would say goodbye to his mom, and walk
towards the porch. Before he could make it to
the landing, Emily would exit the front door and
greet him, waving goodbye to Margherite, lip
synching, "See you in an hour." MarlonDale and
Emily would disappear behind the heavy door.

During these visits, Margherite had taken to
stopping at The Red Door Inn, a nearby
restaurant with a lavish martini menu.
She looked forward to the hour at the Red Door.
She put her mind to sleep.

No thinking, no poetry, no conceptual
relationships to consider. She considered the
irony of her hour, spent in brain cell homicide,
and MarlonDale's constructing new pathways.
Somehow she hoped it would balance.

After disappearing behind the front door,
Emily would escort MarlonDale directly into Dr.
Sutherland's office if she was available. If not, he
was free to go anywhere in the house. He
explored the home and grounds in grid-like
fashion, maintaining a checklist of rooms he had
surveyed, as meticulous and thorough as any
search and rescue team.

The most interesting portions of the home were discovered in his fifth year of therapy. He had completed the search of the grounds in year one and two, discovering two antiquated family cemeteries, one site containing eleven graves dating back to 1810, and the other holding fourteen graves, with dates of death from 1900 to 1945. He told Dr. Sutherland, "Whoever lived on this land has been healthy for 50 years." She laughed.

He also found six wells of various depths. MarlonDale became fascinated with wells and around the age of 17, he journaled an esoteric entry regarding the wells. His journaling, much like his inaudible communication with Dr. Sutherland, was devoid of TenSpeak.

6 January

Thomas Edison said, "Restless is discontent and discontent is the first necessity of progress. Show me a thoroughly satisfied man and I will show you a failure."

I'm restless. I am sure that restlessness is a trait most often ascribed to men of vision. Men whose yearnings exceed those who settle. Never satisfied, always needing more, feeling an emptiness that most certainly can be filled by something, somewhere. Something they yearn for hour by hour day by day.

A hole in their soul that if one just keeps moving, churning through life, shark-like, the fix, the patch will be located. And when one's restlessness points toward fulfillment, it leads to an initial excitatory reaction. Mr. Edison said it was analogous to an erection, so to speak, comparing this sudden burst of innovative clarity, to sex.

This feeling, this arousal, a tocsin for awakening. There is an alertness that is sustained until success. And then the successful pursuit, the hunt, the game is apprehended. The girl is won, the ejaculation complete. The 'AHA' moment when discovery is made, the bass is landed, the deal is closed. The last chapter of a novel savored.

An aura of magnetism and desire switched on. Each victory, a possession for a split second, fills the void, stills the restlessness, but ever so briefly. And there is comfort, stillness, if only for a fleeting second. The man of restlessness savors those moments as much as an addict savors and looks towards his next fix.

Consider a well. A deep, dark, circular red brick hole in the ground. There are four such wells of this type on this property. Each is symmetrically placed at the four corners of the property. I conducted a meticulous search in a 50-meter circumference of each well. No vestiges that any buildings were ever constructed near these wells. The purpose for the wells are unknown and secondary to this entry. Just another noted strange occurrence around here.

The deep brick well. So let's assume the measure of progress is to fill the well. The restlessness can only be abated if the well is filled.

If one places a sphere of some kind, a huge plug of sorts in the well, tightly wedging it in the opening, effectively capping it, to the world, the well no longer exists. It is no longer a dark hole.

Given time and influences from the environment, gaps and cracks develop in the brick and mortar because after all, isn't the well imperfect, having been made by man, not God?

The plug creeps slowly down the well, brick by brick, a lessening of the coefficient of friction, the spaces glide. The plug eventually finds its way to the bottom of the well. It ceases being a plug and becomes part of the well, a new base. The hole once again is real, visual, palpable and the restlessness, the journey, desire to fill the damn thing begins all over again.

There is an Irish proverb, "You never miss the water 'til the well runs dry." I don't think I will ever miss the water because my theoretical well can never be dry.

It is full, full of nothing and seeking to be filled. The monumental task of the relentless seeker is to fill the well from top to bottom, not a little at a time, but all at once.

I am that restless seeker who asks, "Is there a plug big enough to accomplish such a task? A plug that fits from top to bottom. A plug that is infinite and not susceptible to the limitations of time and the imperfections of man."

Surely there must be. Who could make a plug such as this? Who is the plugmaker, the keeper of the plug, capper of restlessness? Could it be God? Is God's purpose to plug my well?

Dr. Sutherland asked MarlonDale what his "well journal" entry meant to him.

MarlonDale said it was one of his deepest journal entries, and smirked, to confirm sending his pun. He said he felt like he was the shark, always alert, swimming, in constant touch with the environment, searching for something with meaning and feeling. A search for his destiny.

MarlonDale said he found Edison's comparison of moments of innovative clarity to sexual relief, fascinating and alluring. He did not feel embarrassed to talk of such things with Dr. Sutherland.

Despite his eccentricities, at that time, MarlonDale was a 17-year-old with a 17-year-old's curiosities and desires. He and Layton had rented some X-rated movies, snuck a few Hustler magazines in the house and even thought about calling an escort service. They had not gone past the thinking stage.

MarlonDale had experienced a few wet dreams. He was bewildered that an ejaculation without physical stimuli could even happen and thought it was an unusual event. It was not necessarily entirely pleasant. In those early morning hours, MarlonDale's brain processed transient enjoyment.

The momentary, wonderful relief was almost immediately coupled with a musty, dank realization of the inner turbulence he felt, a well, his well.

He had Dr. Sutherland as a confidant, a few good friends, including JoHanna Ann, but he was not having sex with either of them. The brevity of satiation from wet dreams or his attempts at masturbation did little to soothe his restlessness.

Dr. Sutherland counseled that the sexual fascinations were normal for a boy his age and that he should experience them with a girl, perhaps JoHanna Ann, if she was equally interested.

During one of the sessions she silently advised, "Marlon, this nomadic agitation to seek, to fulfill, will be realized. Your destiny will be revealed in time. In the interim, I want you to assume a modicum of normality in your actions and desires. We are both quite well aware that this is, and will never be, possible for those like us. But you can, 'act as if' you are normal. Act as if you are one of them. This will pacify the restlessness."

MarlonDale became proficient in "acting as if." He controlled the thigh tapping and the OCD behaviors in public. He appeared near normal to most everyone who did not know him well. Still, MarlonDale needed to find whatever it was that would satisfy his hunger, his craving for completion. The collecting, categorizing, counting, tapping, TenSpeaking, the water towers, and street lamps, all these odd and necessary activities of his childhood and to some degree, the present, they had not plugged the well.

He did not know if the plug would come in the form of a new friend, a girl, an invention, or some type of flabbergasting bombshell discovery he made during his otherwise normal "acting as if" day.

He told Dr. Sutherland that he felt as if whatever it was, was within reach. That with each week, it was as if he was flying in a ship that was traveling in a diminishing circumferential orbit, and when he reached the magnetic center, he would find it.

Dr. Sutherland comforted his concerns, "My dear boy, I understand the impatience you must feel. I promise you will find relief and satisfaction soon enough."

Chapter 24

Y2K, the Millenium and all the fanfare that came with the turn of the calendar was underway when MarlonDale started his weekly sessions with Dr. Sutherland.

At the time, Terry Hendershat and his team had been working on several projects, including a fascinating area of viral vaccine development in hopes of mitigating the problem of MRSA (Methicillin Resistant Staphylococcus Aureus).

The mayor of Kansas City had died of a Staph Aureus infection in early February of 2000. Shortly thereafter, State Representative Martin Woodport entered the Washington University Hospital system in St. Louis with a pneumonia and eventually died of complications resulting from an MSRA infection.

The political knife-wielding and accusations of poor infectious disease control threatened Wash U's hospital accreditation, which had happened briefly in Kansas City after the mayor's death. The governor established a task force to develop a statewide response to the staph infection problem.

To his chagrin, Dr. Hendershat spent too much of his day in conference calls with the governor's staff and/or the hospital board. He was designated the point man to keep everyone up to speed on the issue.

The MRSA claimed the life of Representative Woodport in the first week of March. Patricia Whilder, CEO of the Washington University Hospital systems complex, arranged a meeting with the governor of Missouri, his staff, and a group of about 25 other interested parties, which included influential members of the business community.

Also attending were Patricia's counterparts in the other area hospital systems and a representative from each of the several health departments in Missouri and Illinois.

Patricia Whilder was a formidable looking woman who could have passed for a sister of former U.S. Attorney, Janet Reno. She was an impressive administrator in ways other than mere physical appearance.

She had been with Wash U. for as long as Terry could remember. She started as a nurse, became a nurse administrator, earned her M.S., and an MBA in hospital administration, and climbed the corporate ladder with as much finesse as a fullback picking through a small hole in the front line.

She knew her hospital, her business and her way. She was supportive when things were going well, and a bitch when they weren't. These were bitchy times. Terry had briefed her on several occasions about their viral and MRSA projects. Rather than passively take heat for the MRSA issue, she took this opportunity to showcase how progressive her hospital was, leading the nation, perhaps the world, in innovative disease control. Dr. Hendershat was on point.

Ms. Whilder began, "Governor Culligan and other distinguished guests, thank you for coming to St. Louis. The board, the entire hospital staff is truly saddened by the loss of State Representative Martin Woodport. Martin was a decent, good man and a fine representative to his district. He was a personal friend and a neighbor of mine. Our children attend the same high school and it is indeed a very difficult time for our families as well as our community," she paused and closed her eyes briefly, clearly saddened by the loss. "We are working to refine our capabilities to ensure the health of our patients, while in and out of the hospital, to assure there are no other incidents like Mr. Woodport's or Kansas City Mayor Howell's. We are developing procedures and conducting research that will change the way we, and the world, practice medicine. Martin's family has agreed to allow a discussion of his condition which led to his death. The head of our Infectious Disease Department, Dr. Terry Hendershat, has prepared a briefing for you regarding the death of State Representative Martin Woodport and the important work done on a daily basis by his department. Dr. Hendershat, please."

Terry removed a folded pad of paper from his jacket pocket, opened it up and began his speech. A speech to keep his department running, the hospital accredited, and his job.

"Good morning, Governor Culligan, Ms. Whilder and all of you. Thank you for coming to the hospital," Terry began. "I have spoken with several of you over the last few weeks, since Mr. Woodport's initial admission and his death. I wanted to take this opportunity to provide a more thorough, historical perspective to this disease and what we are currently doing.

Methicillin-Resistant Staphylococcus Aureus (MRSA) infection is caused by Staphylococcus Aureus bacteria — often called "staph." In the late 1980s and early 1990s, a strain of staph emerged in hospitals that was resistant to the broad-spectrum antibiotics commonly used to treat it. It was named Methicillin-Resistant Staphylococcus Aureus (MRSA). It was one of the first germs to outwit all but the most powerful drugs. In worst-case scenarios, MRSA cannot be stopped.

Staph bacteria are normally found on the skin or in the nose of about one-third of the population. If you have staph on your skin or in your nose but aren't sick, you are said to be 'colonized' but not infected with MRSA. Healthy people can be colonized with MRSA and have no ill effects. However, they can pass the germ to others. Some of you in this room are likely 'colonized' carriers, so to speak."

Terry held up his hands in a 'STOP' motion. "Please don't run to the bathroom and start scrubbing, let me finish." He smiled, hoping to break the tension.

"Staph bacteria are generally harmless unless they enter the body through a cut or other wound, and even then they often cause only minor skin problems in healthy people. But in older adults and people who are ill or have weakened immune systems, ordinary staph infections can cause serious illness. In the 1990s, a type of MRSA began showing up in the St. Louis region. Today, that form of staph, known as community-associated MRSA, or CA-MRSA, is responsible for many serious skin and soft tissue infections and for a serious form of pneumonia.

Mr. Woodport presented to our hospital with a pneumonia that he had basically suffered with for nearly two weeks. He was seriously ill when he finally entered our facility. He was subsequently found to have CA-MRSA.

You see, Staph infections, including MRSA, generally start as small red bumps that resemble pimples, boils or spider bites. These can quickly turn into deep, painful abscesses that require surgical draining. Sometimes the bacteria remain confined to the skin. But they can also burrow deep into the body, causing potentially life-threatening infections in bones, joints, surgical wounds, the bloodstream, heart valves and lungs. This is exactly what occurred with Mr. Woodport. He had developed several boils on his legs that were filled with Staph bacteria. The bacteria spread to his lungs, which were more than willing to support the infection.

The bugs, these bacteria, have strong survival skills. They undergo a learning curve as they are treated with a variety of antibiotics and over a long period of time. They can develop an inborn antibiotic resistance to a drug they have consistently recognized. For our current problem, the healthcare community bears most of the responsibility. Like other superbugs, MRSA is the result of decades of excessive and unnecessary antibiotic use. For years, antibiotics have been prescribed for colds, flu and other viral infections that don't respond to these drugs. My generation and the doctors before me, who witnessed the marvels of penicillin, were mesmerized with the power of these drugs to kill the most dreaded diseases they had known.

Having this power in the form of a pill, easily dispensable to anyone who may even remotely appear to suffer from a disease, seemed so easy. And so we prescribed for no reason other than to reassure our patients. And our patients stayed healthy, irregardless of need. We prescribed drugs for simple bacterial infections that normally clear on their own. The bugs have learned and are fighting back.

I cannot place the blame entirely on our physician community. Prescription drugs aren't the only source of antibiotics. In the United States, antibiotics can be found in beef cattle, pigs and chickens. The same antibiotics then find their way into municipal water systems when the runoff from feedlots contaminates streams and groundwater. Routine feeding of antibiotics to animals is banned in the European Union and many other industrialized countries. They have noted that antibiotics given in the proper doses to animals that are actually sick don't appear to produce resistant bacteria. Their zoonotic use is quite judicious compared to the U.S.

I am sure you can appreciate how fast the organic food market, the Trader Joes of the area, are growing in response to this concern.

It is clear that we need to develop tactics to fight infections once they occur that do not involve the use of antibiotics. And we need to offer educational resources to the community so they are able to avoid becoming infected, or at least identify the infection sooner, before aggressive antibiotic therapy is required. Even when antibiotics are used appropriately, they contribute to the rise of drug-resistant bacteria because they don't destroy every germ they target.

Bacteria live on an evolutionary fast track, so germs that survive treatment with one antibiotic soon learn to resist others. And because bacteria mutate much more quickly than new drugs can be produced, some germs end up resistant to just about everything. That's why only a handful of drugs are now effective against most forms of staph."

Terry paused, thankful he did not hear anyone snoring yet.

"I know I have painted a dismal picture of the situation for you. It is very serious, but we are being equally as proactive in our response patterns and are addressing these issues on several fronts.

First, we are identifying the risks for development of MRSA while in the community or if an inpatient at a hospital or long-term facility and then educating our staff, patients and the community. We are identifying at risk patients, enhancing our use of hygiene practices and using antibiotic therapy judiciously. We are also researching a number of alternatives for managing a staph infection without antibiotics

So the question is, what else can we do to avoid another Martin Woodport-type death? Here at Wash U. we've been working on a revolutionary and exciting research project for nearly two years.

Our research was initiated to combat viral infections such as HIV and viral hepatitis, and will have great utility in the event of a cyclical pandemic flu. A surprising find was that the Virotic Program, that's the name of our research program, The Virotics Program, has shown very good results in combating bacterial infections, including MRSA. We believe we are on the cusp of a new frontier for disease and infection control. I don't want to bore you or get overly technical, but please allow me a moment to give you a little background. It will make Virotics much easier to understand."

Terry's assistant dimmed the lights and their power point presentation began with a multidimensional and colorful slide of viruses.

"When a foreign substance invades the body, the immune system activates certain cells to destroy the invader. These cells recognize the foreign invader and kill it, but unfortunately, the infected cell dies. Too many infected cells die, we may die. Fortunately, the cells from the immune system have a memory and can remember the foreigner the next time it invades the body and responds more vigorously to keep us from getting sick."

Terry couldn't see past the bright light of the powerpoint projector, but he imagined that people were looking at their watches or otherwise bored to death.

"Viruses use a 'Trojan horse' strategy to enter cells. The virus has a coat so to speak, that has specific sites that will fit specifically onto a healthy cell in order to infect it. It is an exact fit, much like those children's toys in which the triangle-shaped piece can only fit into the triangle opening. The healthy cell thinks since it is an exact fit, it must be ok. The virus waits for the cell to make the fatal mistake of actively transporting the virus inside, triangle piece into triangle hole. Once inside, the virus will take over the genetic material in the cell and uses the cell as a factory to replicate more virus, essentially killing the host cell. So, where are we going with this? " No response from the audience as expected.

Terry continued, "In the early 1990s, a novel antiviral drug named Glymetphelin was synthesized. Glymetphelin inhibits the formation of the protective protein coat, called a capsid, that a virus needs. It is on this coat that the specific receptor docking sites are located, the triangle shapes. No coat, no sites, no docking to a healthy cell and thus, no spread of the virus.

The mechanism of action revealed that Glymetphelin docked with a drug-binding pocket within the capsid, the coat, and interacted with the amino acids of a particular capsid protein. Glymetphelin was especially effective against most rhinoviruses, those causing the common cold, but was not as effective as hoped against HIV. It was good for your sniffles, seasonal flu. However, an unexpected effect of Glymetphelin was that it altered the amino acid sequence of immature healthy cells to that resembling the structure of morphine."

Terry paused and stepped in front of the podium. He looked around the dim conference room. Several had closed their eyes, a few were leaning over whispering. This was way too boring for this crowd. He was losing them. But, not Patricia Whilder. She was focused on the slides, her head looking up and then down towards a legal pad where she scribbled notes.

"I realize this has been very technical. I'm almost finished," Terry said.

A few faces smiled, a few coughs, a few looked up at the slides.

"In human clinical trials, providing small doses of Glymetphelin stopped the viral replication, basically killing the cold virus, while larger doses put immature cells, for lack of a better term, to sleep," Terry said. "At the time, researchers did not pursue the benefit of the reduced immature cell activity. When we noticed this morphine like result from Glymetphelin, our team took an extra step. This resting immature cell, the cell that is asleep, appears at this point in our research, impenetrable by any of the viruses I mentioned a moment ago, HIV, Hepatitis. We hypothesized that because the metabolic processes of the cell are significantly inhibited, slowed, sleeping, hibernating, the invading virus is unable to survive long enough to find an awake host cell to enter and cause disease. And while they are asleep, the immature cells glean an immunity to the invader. We treat the mature, awake cells normally, as we would with antivirals, antibiotics, basically buying time and allowing the body to build resistance, immunity. We also developed a metabolic enhancer to hasten the maturity of the immature, sleeping cells. As these cells mature and wake up, they maintain their resistance to some of the worst viral infectious agents.

The basic concept is somewhat analogous to early chemotherapy and radiation therapy. Both therapies were designed to kill the patient's cells. Our hopes then were that the weaker cancer cells succumbed first, before too many of the patient's healthy cells died, potentially ending the patient's life.

The Virotics project does not harm healthy cells, just puts them to sleep. And during that time period, we fight the virus traditionally and a lot of the virus dies. The new cells cannot be infected and the remaining virus dies. Our research is very promising and we hope to begin human clinical trials later this year. With appropriate funding from the government, and of course a little luck, we anticipate the development of a Virotic vaccine capable of narcotizing cells which in turn, when mature, will be resistant to a number of viruses and bacteria, including MRSA. It is probably the most exciting advancement in our generation. I would be happy to answer any questions you may have. Thank you."

Chapter 25

Despite the dryness and technicality of the presentation, at least the attendees were satisfied that Ms. Whilder and Wash U were taking appropriate action. The governor's chief of staff, Mark McClanahan, was a physician in a pre-political life, and took particular note of Virotics. Mark was a diminutive man who reminded Terry of George Stephanopolous, President Bill Clinton's one-time chief of staff. Mark McClanahan was genuinely interested in the Virotic project.

In the weeks that followed, Dr. McClanahan and Terry corresponded often as Terry fully explained the Virotic hypothesis. Mark was impressed with the work and the initial success of Virotics.

He confided in Terry that he had been diagnosed with HIV and was taking the most recent cocktail of medications to curtail any progression to active AIDS. He was intimately hopeful that Glymetphelin worked as advertised.

Dr. McClanahan's brother, Mike, happened to be the second in command at the FDA. Using some well-heeled contacts and calling in some markers, Mike McClanahan was able to help the Virotics project at Wash U push through the federal bureaucracy.

Glymetphelin was already designated as an Investigational New Drug. The previous research concerning its ability to elicit a protective immune response (immunogenicity) and its safety in animal testing was already established. The proposed clinical protocol relative to the cellular narcosis for studies in humans was described.

With Mike McClanahan's assistance, the governmental paper shuffling was nearly effortless. Clinical trials for vaccines, drugs or biologics are typically done in three phases with increasing numbers of human subjects in each phase, closely monitored to identify the benefit or harm the drug provides

In the fall of 2001, they were well into Phase 2 with excellent results. Mark McClanahan had volunteered and was responding as expected. His HIV titre decreased and his immunologist was considering reducing the cocktail drugs. Terry postulated that by early 2003, they should be able to make application for their Biological Licensing Agent which moved Glymetphalin closer to the market.

He hoped during the next two years that they would be able to identify additional specific markers on the viral cell surface that could enable them to target the virus itself with a narcotizing Virotic agent rather than merely the immature cells. This was a busy time for Terry Hendershat.

Chapter 26

Just like nearly everyone else, Terry Hendershat's world changed at 7:45 a.m. Central time on September 11, 2001, when a hijacked passenger jet, American Airlines Flight 11 out of Boston, Massachusetts, crashed into the north tower of the World Trade Center. At 8:03 a.m., a second hijacked airliner, United Airlines Flight 175 from Boston, crashed into the south tower. American Airlines Flight 77 struck the Pentagon at 9:37 a.m. and United Flight 93 crashed in a Pennsylvania farm field at 9:57 a.m.

Terry and Margherite had just dropped MarlonDale off at school, where he was mainstreaming, thanks to Mac Sutherland. Margherite was taking Terry to the airport as he was scheduled to meet Mike McClanahan and present an update to the FDA in Washington on the Virotic project. Terry had to pick up a file at Saint Louis University's School of Public Health, so they found themselves downtown that early fall morning.

For old times' sake, they decided to run by the Eat Rite Diner on Choteau Avenue for breakfast. Terry occasionally ate lunch at the landmark restaurant.

The Eat Rite had been home base at one time or another to nearly everyone who had ever closed down a bar and stumbled down city streets in search of grub. Drunk students, the homeless, occasional celebrities, all sitting on plastic covered stools around the dining counter at 2 a.m., gobbling a plateful of eggs and chili, a 'Slinger,' so named because the cook slung the chili over raw eggs on the grill. There were no tables or four-legged chairs.

A juke box, cigarette machine and pinball were the only amenities, aside from the diners. The crusty 400-square-foot diner became trendy as the downtown area grew. They sold T-shirts that advertised "Eat Rite, or Don't Eat at All."

Margherite hadn't been there in years, since before the boys. A time when she and Terry seemed to talk freely, and have fun. Before MarlonDale, before her popcorn puppies and yoga, art, profanity poetry readings. Terry drank more often then. Now, she put away enough for the both of them.

That morning, September 11, 2001, a 12-inch black and white television set with dial controls sat atop the 5-cent, "Happy Days" pinball machine in the corner. Margherite recalled that TV, or one just like it, had been there 20 years earlier.

Katie Couric was reading a news story about the Middle East when she suddenly stopped the story, cleared her throat and read the news concerning the first plane striking the World Trade Center.

There were two other patrons in the Eat Rite at the time. The "Hamburger Guy", as Terry identified him, and an overweight woman in surgical clothing. Judging by the Winnie-the-Pooh scrubs, probably a night shift nurse from Children's Hospital.

The Hamburger Guy was a local homeless man who wandered the city and could be seen almost anywhere, from Uncle Bill's in South City, to the Pasta House in the Chesterfield Mall. Hamburger Guy was almost apparitional. He could be standing nearby one minute, a physical and olfactory assault. Look away for a second, and he would have silently vanished. He was a tall, thin, black man, probably in his 50s with a full, bushy, salt and pepper beard. His left eye was totally obscured with a crystalline blue, opaque cataract.

He walked with a slight limp and shuffle, wearing oversized high top tennis shoes without laces. All year round he wore a dark wool navy Peacoat. He had earned his name by standing outside the Wash U clinical labs demanding, "I need a dollar for a hamburger," from the exiting staff.

Terry was a soft touch for the homeless and gave the Hamburger Guy a dollar whenever he saw him which was at least a couple dozen times over the past 2-3 years. Nevertheless, there was no recognition on the Hamburger Guy's face as he looked up at Terry and Margherite when they entered the Eat Rite.

The first person to say anything after Katie read the story was Oscar, the grill cook. "Son of a bitch, can't them damn pilots see a damn building. The towers are about as big as a mountain. I remember when my cousin Al flew a crop duster. He clipped a grain silo, tore the hell out of the plane and a corn field. He had a drinking problem though, so it wasn't like it was a big surprise or anything. But this one, man oh man, somebody's going to get their ass sued, I swear to God they are."

Betty the waitress said in a "Kiss My Grits" drawl, "Oscar, hush up. I wanna hear the news, now shut your pie hole."

A few minutes later, the report of the second plane crash, and the printing of history books had to stop to collect their thoughts.

All airline travel was cancelled at 8:40 a.m. Terry paid for their uneaten Slingers and Margherite drove Terry home. Margherite spent the entire day in front of the TV, entranced by the magnitude of the day, and making microwave popcorn.

Terry went to work. He tried calling Mark's brother in Washington, D.C., but no one at the FDA answered their phones. All federal buildings were being evacuated. At 9:59 a.m., the south tower collapsed, and at 10:28 a.m., the north tower fell. The script for a new era in U.S. history was being written. Nothing ever would be the same.

Sure, drunks would still find respite with an Eat Rite slinger at 2 a.m. But the feeling of confidence, safety and security in the power of the United States of America would never be the same. The nation had been attacked, its citizens murdered, on its own shores, by foreigners. America was under attack.

Chapter 27

Dr. Hendershat's lab and clinic were located on the fourth floor of the new Cancer Research Center on Forest Park Boulevard, in the center of the Barnes-Jewish-Washington University Hospital Complex. The building was buff brick with mirrored windows and shiny stainless bracing. The front entrance was concave and seemed to exude an increase in gravitational pull, as if going down a steep hill.

MarlonDale loved to watch the building as it was under construction, the shiny windows and shiny steel. And the lighting for the entire area was nicely accomplished with newly-minted vintage-styled Westinghouse Silverliners, Mercury Vapor Lamps.

The building was ten stories tall and housed several hundred physicians. It housed oncologists, hematologists, radiologists, surgeons, and the most advanced and expensive imaging and diagnostic services in the state.

In quite a few university settings, research laboratories generally are relegated to loading dock or basement digs, but Patricia Whilder would have none of that. She was well aware that research requires funding, funding creates growth and growth creates wealth and power. The funding for the research came from private and public sources.

Wealthy private donors who had been cured at the old Cancer Center, realizing the need for additional research facilities, and thankful to be alive, helped her build the Taj Mahal of Wash U. Her foresight in providing a first-class facility for treatment and research fostered the respect she deserved from her physicians and the business community.

Terry parked the Volvo in the attached parking garage, walked to the lobby and took the elevator. He normally used the stairs. It typically was the only cardio exercise in which he participated. But on this day, 9/11, his strength and will was zapped.

Terry swiped his ID badge, placed his thumb over the biometric sensor and entered the lab through the employee door at the end of the hallway. Elaine and Mary, graduate medical students working in Infectious Disease, were crying next to the TV in the break room.

Terry listened as Elaine repeatedly dialed her cell phone, trying to reach her younger brother Don, who worked for Empire Blue Cross Blue Shield with offices in the World Trade Center. She muttered, "Dammit, God damn phones" several times.

Elaine had been working for Terry in ID for almost two years and was the brightest and most intuitive of doctors he had worked with in years, despite her youth. She undoubtedly was going places and her time at Wash U would be just a stopover towards some measure of greatness.

As is often the case, her brilliance was not matched by her attention to appearance. She rarely took time to apply makeup or do her hair. She wore frumpy, comfortable clothes under her lab coat. She was very down to Earth. Had it been the '60s, she would have worn Earth shoes, but now they were called Crocks.

Terry put on his lab coat.

"It is incomprehensible," Terry said. "Both towers gone, thousands must have perished. I don't know if I can concentrate fully today," he said half to himself. "How are you both doing?"

Mary answered first. "I can't pull myself away from the TV. It's like watching a trainwreck, I just can't stop. It is disgustingly mesmerizing, watching the towers crumble."

Mary's voice trembled as she pulled a Kleenex out of the box and dabbed her eyes. She looked up at the clock.

"Oh, gosh, Dr. Hendershat, I have to bring back a few patients for workups," Mary said.

Terry put a hand on Mary's shoulder to settle her.

"It's alright," Terry said. "We're all in this together. The patient's will be upset, too. Let's just take it slow today, OK, doctors?"

Mary nodded her head unconvincingly, grabbed a few patient charts and left the room.

"Any luck in getting through, Elaine?" Terry asked.

"Not, uh, not yet, all the cell phone circuits are locked up," Elaine replied. "He lives in Queens and I called his apartment and spoke to his roommate. He was pretty sure Don would have gone to work, but he said Don spent the night at Theresa's apartment in Brooklyn. So, he didn't know and I really don't know."

Elaine started sobbing. Terry put his arm around her and held her for a few moments.

Elaine finally got in touch with her brother. He had spent the night at his girlfriend's and had taken the day off work. However, Elaine said he had lost 7 very close friends at Blue Cross on 9/11.

The ID department and the Virotics lab conducting the human trials were going well, funding was adequate and people were getting healthy. Normally, this would have been a time of celebration and promise. But there was nothing normal.

There was a tangible melancholy amongst the entire staff that seemed endless.

Chapter 28

Terry Hendershat was the first to admit that of all the infectious disease physicians in the country, he would be the last to be called upon by the government. He was a busy clinician, a researcher on a fascinating and astonishing project, but he was not a government player. He liked the academia, the liberal atmosphere, the free thinking.

The government always felt repressive and taxing in both senses of the word. He had a dysfunctional family, no hobbies or diversions from work, and as a result, a mild depression, which he self-treated with a combination selective serotonin reuptake inhibitor/norepinephrine selective reuptake inhibitor. The combo kept him from driving the Volvo off a bridge or having an affair with Mac Sutherland, either of which appealed to him on occasion, in comparison to his home life.

However, as the events surrounding 9/11 developed, and Anthrax became a household word, specialists in infectious disease and Dr. Terry Hendershat, became quite fashionable and necessary.

Letters contaminated with a weapons-grade Anthrax appeared at the Senate Building and NBC headquarters beginning on September 18, 2001. Over the next few months, five people would die from the Anthrax contamination and 17 would become sick.

Terry received a phone call from Mike McClanahan on September 20.

"Terry, hello. How are you?" Mike said in cordial tone, a hollow, emptiness resonating behind the words.

"Mike, hi. Umm, how are you, are you OK? I feel so bad about things," Terry asked.

"Yea, it's difficult and different. We lost some good people. Everything is evolving and changing. I think entropy would best describe things," Mike said.

"You know, I was on my way to the airport for our meeting when they closed air travel," Terry said. "I called your office a few times, but decided that everyone in D.C. was totally involved with too many things. I am a bit surprised you have the time to call St. Louis. But, our project is going well, following the path we discussed at the last phone conference."

"Very exciting stuff you have going, exciting stuff," Mike said, his voice again dropping off a cliff, missing heartbeats. "Terry, I, we, would like for you to come up here right away. The Anthrax attacks have us considering worst-case scenarios. We know there are tons of the worst possible bugs out there on the open market. I am not telling you anything you cannot find on the Internet. Iraq, Iran, the former Soviet Union. Christ, everyone had a biologic program."

Mike continued, "In the friggin 80s, when Iraq was an ally, we supplied them with biologics for research, for Chrissake. Terry, the government has some real concerns about Anthrax and Smallpox, Tularemia, Plague, Marburg, E Bola, and others. We could use some help by someone who is an ID guy, and your specialty and research are what we need."

"Thanks for those kind words, Mike," Terry said. "I, uh, I attended a couple conferences on Category A agent Bioterrorism diseases last year. Scary stuff, to be sure. You know we have a very robust biological terrorism program at St. Louis University. It really is frightening to know those bugs are out there in someone's warehouse. Frightening."

"Terry, we had a brainstorming meeting yesterday with the State Department, FDA, CDC, and all the other Justice Department alphabet agencies, and the President," Mike said. "Virotics came up, your name came up."

Terry leaned back in his chair and put his feet up on the desk.

"I think I know where you are going," Terry said rubbing his forehead, "and I guess it is possible that Glymetphelin could mitigate biological viral agents, but we haven't tested anything that aggressive and deadly. I guess, aside from HIV patients. Not even active AIDS at this point. I don't know if the immature cells could be enhanced rapidly enough to combat a really aggressive, overwhelming biologic attack."

"Terry, I've read your clinical phase reports and it is clearly strong information," Mike said. "The President would like you and if you need some help, a few of your people, to assist in formulating our response plan to intentional terrorism with a deadly organism. Not that Virotics is the answer, just that it is something that should be considered. It will probably be a six-month assignment. We'll work out all the details with Ms. Whilder, Patricia, right? Your salary, housing, benefit package, admin staffing, trips back home on some weekends. Or if you like, trips for the family to visit you while you are in D.C. We will make it as easy for you and your family as possible. These are trying times, I know. Do you think that is possible?" Mike asked, his last sentence, desert flat, without an upward inflection indicative of a question.

"Wow, not what I expected to be talking to you about. I am a little stunned. How soon do you have to know?" Terry asked.

Mike answered, "This think tank is being established as we speak and the other players will be here One, October. Let me know as soon as you can, early next week. Keep on with Phase 2 in the meantime. I have to go, call me anytime."

Chapter 29

Terry moved to Washington, D.C., where he spent the next eight months in discussions with the best and brightest from the CDC and a dozen other hospitals and universities. A consensus on a response pattern for contagious biological diseases was formulated and distributed throughout the United States. Terry continued to direct the Virotic Project at Wash U. Elaine conducted her form of shuttle diplomacy, working with Terry two weeks assisting with the team in DC, and two weeks at the lab carrying out Terry's directions.

Terry was gone from home for 8 months and returned home in March 2002. During the time in Washington, D.C., Margherite visited three times and the boys came for five weekends. There were no additional bioterrorism attacks. A semblance of safety was returning to the nation.

The Virotic Project had run into a few snags. The process was effective for common flu, viral Hepatitis, viral pneumonia, MRSA, and Smallpox, and showed promise in limiting the growth of the Anthrax, Tularemia, Plague and the hemorrhagic fevers. There was more work to be done.

The studies indicated that Virotics were effective for diseases with an incubation period less than 10 days or in those patients who exhibited symptoms of infection rapidly. The key was in getting the patient the Glymetphelin before there were an overwhelming number of invader cells. The fly in the ointment was that the metabolic enhancer could not increase the rate of maturity of the protected cells rapidly enough when faced with a racing, fulminant, infection. In Terry's mind, that was like eating double crème-filled Oreos with skim soy milk.

As far as the governor and Patricia Whilder were concerned, managing MRSA and common flu were successes. The fact that Terry and Elaine assisted the government in the development of a program to enhance the country's ability to respond to a biological terror attack was icing on the cake and certainly helped with re-election, grants and salary negotiations, respectively.

Terry moved from his fifteen minutes of fame and back to normality. And the next 8 years passed by like a day. Margherite had progressed from popcorn puppies to a number of other artistic oddities. Currently, it was appliance box painting. She and the boys would obtain the large cardboard boxes from appliance or hardware stores, strap them to the top of the Infiniti SUV that she drove, and bring them home.

Margherite had the boys seal her in the box with her paints. Totally taped, sealed in, claustrophobically, totally dark. Margherite was indeed claustrophobic. It was a terribly uncomfortable artistic endeavor. She explained that the fear went into the paint.

In a maddening, frenetic ten-minute dash in the box, Margherite screamed, threw, drew, spit and rubbed paint on all six sides of the interior of the box. After ten minutes, the boys let her out. MarlonDale acted as if he were David Copperfield, graciously extending his hand to help his assistant from the box. Margherite, covered with adrenalin, paint, sweat and saliva, would exit as fashionably as Cinderella stepping out of the pumpkin carriage for the dance, and promptly vomit into a nearby bucket. And, of course, the boxes were titled, displayed and explained at Barnes and Nobles during Impressionist Week.

Terry continued to self-medicate.

Chapter 30

MarlonDale graduated from high school. With Dr. Sutherland's counseling, he essentially appeared to be a normal young man. The visible expressions of his Aspergers Disorder were under control for the most part. He rarely thigh tapped, unless he became very nervous or tense. He attended a large high school and his TenSpeak went unnoticed.

MarlonDale had a few friends whom he kept close all through middle and high school. Two of his best friends also became Dr. Sutherland's patients.

JoHanna Ann Steinburgh, MarlonDale's best friend, was diagnosed with Aspergers a few years after he had been. JoHanna Ann had an IQ of 165 and, like most geniuses and Aspies, she exhibited quirks in behavior and action. She had a noticeable head tic, in which about every 6 seconds, her head bobbed down and to the right. She was impulsive and easily distracted and had considerable difficulty focusing while at school. JoHanna had been treated with medication for ADHD, prior to her sessions with Dr. Sutherland. JoHanna Ann was obsessed with orderliness, blueprints, structure, crop circles and like Marlondale, astronomy. JoHanna Ann had difficulty remaining still, taking turns, and keeping quiet.

She was the most clumsy of MarlonDale's Aspie friends and visited the Hendershats with a new bruise on her shins or forehead nearly every week from a fall or a wrong turn into a wall or fence.

JoHanna Ann lived with her mother, Roberta. Roberta had been left a sizable annuity upon the death of her husband years ago from a sudden heart attack. She used a considerable portion of the money to assure JoHanna Ann received the best care. Noting the improvement in MarlonDale's social skills, Roberta asked Terry and Margherite what was responsible for the change. Once learning about Dr. McAllister Sutherland, she enrolled her daughter in the program. The two Aspies were inseparable.

JoHanna Ann and MarlonDale could have been confused as boyfriend-girlfriend, although neither Terry, Margherite or Roberta had an inkling as to whether they were ever intimate. The two of them made a fine looking pair. MarlonDale was 5-foot-10, 170 pounds with dark, thick hair like his mothers', a slender muscular build from years of swimming, the one sport in which he was able to excel. It was quiet, wet, anti-gravity like, sleek. He felt at home in water. And at water towers.

JoHanna Ann was thin, with an angular jaw, much like Dr. Sutherland's. She kept her auburn hair short and occasionally dyed it bright red. She was curvaceous despite her leanness. Her breasts were a little larger than one would have expected for her diminutive frame. MarlonDale found her physically appealing.

Truth be told, JoHanna Ann and MarlonDale had engaged in sexual prelims, but it felt strange, almost like they were siblings. And as they would later learn, there was a reason they sensed something odd.

While waiting for their appointments to normalize their neuronal flow, JoHanna Ann and MarlonDale often would roam Dr. Sutherland's house and grounds, discovering its intricacies.

JoHanna Ann had sketched detailed plans of Dr. Sutherland's old house, using a 25-foot measuring tape and taking everything to scale on a legal size paper. Over the years, she had accumulated an entire notebook of handmade blueprints of Dr. Sutherland's home.

Roberta and Margherite had become close friends during the years in which they would drop the kids off and pick them up. They frequented a nearby lounge, the Red Door, as well as a number of other bars within a few miles of Dr. Sutherland's clinic.

Between the alcohol, raising two teenage boys, September 11, 2001, Terry's absence, and the depression, Margherite felt as if a silent thief had pilfered the past 8 years. She was glad to have found a friend.

Chapter 31

As far as Dr. Sutherland knew, MarlonDale had not let anyone in on his Mercury Vapor Experiences. She felt that they had kept a secret bond concerning this revelation and their secret was secure.

Shortly after his 20th birthday, MarlonDale experienced an MVE that included JoHanna Ann, and the secret was no longer shared only by two. MarlonDale and JoHanna Ann were returning from late afternoon classes at the Community Junior College. He had begun taking classes in preparation for a degree in electrical engineering. JoHanna Ann was taking coursework dedicated to architecture.

They both planned to switch to a four-year college.

They and their parents were well aware of the challenges college level work would bring.

However, Dr. Sutherland assured all of them that MarlonDale and JoHanna Ann were equipped for any coursework they would encounter.

So far, her words of encouragement were accurate. They both were doing well and had each accumulated 36 hours of credit, taking the same preparatory basic courses. They had parallel disorders, parallel lives. The major differences were JoHanna Ann's bruises, and MarlonDale's continued street lamp obsession.

"Hurry up JoHanna Ann, it's getting dark, come on already," Marlon pleaded. "Come on, hurry, will you, should I just carry you?" MarlonDale asked, walking hurriedly up his driveway from the garage where he parked the Volvo his father had passed on to him. The 1988 model with 187,000 was still running fine.

"If I hurry, I fall, we take longer, you don't get to see the lights come on, and I have to hear about it," JoHanna Ann said as her head bobbed down and then angled back up.

MarlonDale and JoHanna Ann quickly walked up the ten steps of the Hendershat porch, a feat accomplished without a JoHanna Ann injury. The porch ran across the entire front of the house and along the east side. Terry had it replaced a few years earlier with plastic decking. MarlonDale did not necessarily like the artificial feel of the plastic, however, it did not require maintenance and neither he or Layton had to powerwash or reseal it. "Convenience versus aesthetics" is what Margherite disapprovingly called the plastic porch.

Two lawn chairs were awaiting MarlonDale's and JoHanna Ann's arrival.

With time to spare, they sat down. JoHanna Ann rose and said she was going to go in and get them a blanket.

As she opened the screen door, she stepped in acutely, turning too early. She banged her knee on the inside edge of the door frame.

"Dammit, first bruise today. I actually thought I was going to go a whole day," JoHanna Ann said.

"Get a bag of frozen peas out of the fridge. And, if there are any Dr. Peppers, bring them out," Marlon said.

JoHanna Ann had been with MarlonDale on a number of occasions when the Mercury Vapor Lamps lit. For everyone but MarlonDale, the only result was a hazy illumination of the neighborhood. This was her time for normal to change.

JoHanna Ann sat down in her lawn chair and balanced the bag of frozen peas on her knee. She handed MarlonDale a Dr. Pepper. JoHanna took a drink from hers, dribbling a few brown drops onto her chin. Marlon noticed, and motioned with his finger at her chin. She raked her forearm across and wiped the soda. She shifted in her chair and the peas fell to the floor.

"Look, look, look JoHanna, the flicker, the flicker, the light," Marlon said, the tone of his voice rising with excitement and anticipation. The same thrill and shiver he'd felt his entire life as the Silverliner's fired up, coursed down his spine.

It never got old for him.

Chapter 32

As soon as the MV light became steady, the street peeled back like a blanket and folded over itself again and again and again, rolling up like a licorice roll avalanche. No remnant of roadway could be seen, only the fresh ground that lay beneath the street. Despite the chaotic activity, the environment was completely silent.. The cool evening became a balmy 80 degrees.

The reality that Mercury Vapor produced for MarlonDale, included for lack of a better description, silvery beings. Aliens, Extra Terrestrials of some order.

The beings, the repairmen, as MarlonDale called them, popped vertically out of the ground where the road had been, much like a 'Jack in the Box' except there was no music.

The bag of frozen peas made a crunch when they fell to the porch floor. MarlonDale looked to JoHanna Ann. Her mouth was agape. Marlon had never seen her eyes so wide. He loved her eyes.

Her irises, the color of a light green Demantoid crystal, sparkled as they reflected the flickering Silverliners. Her Adams Apple bounced up and down like a tennis ball as she tried to comprehend and speak at the same time, a task that was temporarily impossible.

"I call them the repairmen because they fix the lights," Marlon said to break the silence.

JoHanna gulped down Dr. Pepper. More dribbling down the chin, which this time, Marlon wiped away with his sleeve.

"We're really seeing this? This is really happening. It's not bad popcorn or Dr. Pepper, or, geez, I don't know what," JoHanna Ann asked.

Marlon leaned over and picked up the peas. He placed them back on her knee and held them there.

"Well, well, well, welcome to my world JoHanna Ann Steinburgh," Marlon said.

With his other hand, he took hold of one of hers. Their fingers interlaced. It was warm. Holding hands with JoHanna felt comfortable.

They watched in silence. JoHanna Ann was still spellbound. They could see them and hear them, but could not interact.

The shiny beings were similar in appearance to the typical googlcable alien.

The repairmen were of small stature with spindly extremities and large heads. The shiny beings made noises, a high-pitched whine interspersed with a grunting sound. Perhaps it was speech. There was nothing discernable to Marlon or JoHanna, and it clearly was not an Earthly language.

MarlonDale spoke softly and repeated, "I call them the repairmen because they fix the lamps."

JoHanna Ann was silent. Her grip on Marlon's hand increased.

"MarlonDale Hendershat. This is totally awesome, incredible, fantabulous," JoHanna Ann said.

"JoHanna, do you notice that they are wearing outerwear, clothes? Most aliens don't wear clothes, do they now JoHanna, right?" Marlon asked. "Can you guess why, especially with the environment so temperate? Can you guess why sophisticated aliens need to wear clothes?"

JoHanna Ann watched the shiny people shimmy up the light pole. Within a minute , the flickering lamp was exchanged. Her head bobbed up and down several times with one sharp jag to the right.

She thought for a moment. "Marlon, these, well whatever they are, you say they are the Tom Vila galactical repairmen," JoHanna Ann said.

"They have to have tools to fix whatever it is that they fix, the bulbs or whatever. Where would they put their tools? Even for aliens in a weird, alternate reality, it helps to have pockets."

MarlonDale smiled and nodded his head. She got it.

Over the years, MarlonDale had not totally understood what they were doing, why they were there. He recognized one of their assignments, when they changed a malfunctioning MV light. But sometimes, they just popped up, zipped away, and then popped in. What they did, why they were here, on his street, on every street lit by a Mercury Vapor Lamp, was a conundrum.

JoHanna Ann and MarlonDale watched as the repairmen popped out of the ground and did whatever they needed to do to the street lamps. A few who were not working would move in and out of sight with a sparkly comet-like tail following them. And in some respects, the repairmen were like union employees. One working, three or four watching.

There was no way of calculating time, but eventually the Shinies blended vertically back into the ground.

"Wow," JoHanna Ann said as each one disappeared below ground, a sprinkle of fairy dust following them. "It's like the Transporter on Star Trek, all sparkles and wavy, then gone."

The roadway had not yet returned. The damp smell of fresh dirt flittered by.

"There have been a few benefits of this weird operation," MarlonDale said. "Large street cracks or potholes get fixed during the process. Layton and I really appreciated that riding skateboards and bikes."

MarlonDale told JoHanna Ann that he had witnessed this Mercury Vapor Experience thousands of times, the road rolling, Shinies shimmying, sparkles waving, repairs made. He told her that was the usual order of things. Until the night he almost froze to death. That night was different from all the other nights.

"On that particular night, I was invited to go underground," MarlonDale said.

Chapter 32

On that night, ten years ago, Layton and Margherite had just gone inside. He was only to stay out 10 minutes. Margherite went in the house to pop popcorn, drink martinis and forget about her 10-year-old Aspie son sitting out on the porch in 20 degree weather. As they always did, the street lights flickered, the steady stream of vapor appeared, and the streets rolled back like a Yo-Yo. The repairmen popped up. Many of them immediately went elsewhere, glistening trails of sparkle and wave following them.

On that occasion, a decade ago, two of them dressed in shiny clothes with what looked like wrenches and screwdrivers in their pockets, walked across the lawn, away from the street light, towards MarlonDale's house. MarlonDale sat on the edge of his lawn chair, head craning forward, mouth hanging open. His breath was no longer smoky frost. The air felt different, heavy, but very warm. As they approached he understood them.

There were no words spoken, all communication muted. MarlonDale immediately recognized the TenSpeak.

"Only a special few may notice as we arrive here. You are one of the special, please come with us."

MarlonDale took a deep breath in and exhaled loudly. His fingers tapped his thigh faster than a Ginger Baker drum roll. And with that, he was no longer on the porch, but was standing on the ground where the street in front of his house used to be, where his chalk line for free throws to his basketball hoop had been. And then descent.

He had a stomach-turning feeling as rapid as any Six Flags roller coaster he had ever ridden. And then a stop, as smooth as the elevator in Dad's hospital.

MarlonDale arrived to find himself immersed in an aqueous cavernous area.

He was definitely not standing on a firm surface and he felt suspended like a marionette in the environment. It was like being in the deep end of the pool.

He could move about unencumbered. There was no end to the cavern in any direction, if that is what it was. The air was not as heavy as it had been above ground and the temperature was quite a bit warmer, late July or August-like.

He took off his parka, wrapping the arms around his waist and tying them together in front so he would not have to carry it.

There were structures of a variety of shapes and sizes. Several were wide and as tall as an office building complex.

Others were only one or two levels. The conformations of the buildings were not fixed, more like plasmic and liquid. They maintained their basic anatomy and shape but looked as if they had the pulpy, gooey consistency of hair gel.

MarlonDale envisioned that he had traveled to a type of city on a distant planet or an entirely different reality deep within the Earth, a Journey to the Center of the Earth world.

There was a bright, crisp, clean white light, just like Mercury Vapor emissions, bathing the entire area, although he could not see the source of the light. MarlonDale made note that the buildings did not cast any shadows.

There was activity. Hundreds of Shinies were milling about. In and out of the structures, as if this was a Monday morning.

As he moved about in the goo, MarlonDale hadn't noticed that the two repairmen, the ones with tools who had invited him on this trip, had vanished.

A majority of the Shinies he now saw did not wear clothes. MarlonDale figured that even in this reality there were blue collar workers, those who worked with their hands and tools, and white collar workers who didn't.

MarlonDale tried moving about in the serous gel and found that he had considerable freedom. Jumping up, he was able to travel at least twice his height.

Four or five jumps later, someone spoke to him.

"I see you have discovered a property of our environment. A trampoline, correct, jumping, denying gravitational forces as it were?" a white collar Shiny said, with an accent not quite English, more Australian. He was tall and gangly. A seven-foot, skinny silver Gumby, with long hands and fingers.

"Yea, I guess so, um, so, uh, where am I?" MarlonDale said out loud, as he thigh tapped nervously.

The being spoke verbally as well. "We can do without the TenSpeak here, MarlonDale. The TenSpeak is only used above the crust level It was designed as a way for the special ones to acknowledge each other.

You are perfectly capable and we actually would urge you to speak audibly, if you like, or telepathically. Use as many words to form sentences as you like down here. The decimal system, and all that 010101 computer code your species developed to foster common scientific communication and understanding, it is irrelevant here. Speak freely, be verbose, enjoy your language," the Shiny said, smiling widely, extending his arms to the sides, as if he were a game show host opening up door number three. "And you do not have to resort to any of those other coping behaviors, thigh tapping, obsessive collecting, being so orderly down here, either. Those quirks were more of the behaviors to help bring you, who live above the crust, to identify each other, bring you to the each other and eventually here."

The Shiny said this with a hint of impatience and boredom.

"What do you mean there are others? Other, who others?" MarlonDale asked, as his thigh tapping and TenSpeak melted away.

"Marlon, and we can just use Marlon. We don't need to continue to use MarlonDale either," the Shiny said. "Have you noticed that your name is ten letters, M one, A, two, R, three, L, four, O, five, N, six, D, seven, A, eight, L, nine, E, ten? And how about your last name, too? HENDERSHAT, count it out. And how about your mother's name, MARGHERITE, ten letters?"

MarlonDale chewed the inside of his lip, thinking about that. "You mean my Mom, she is another special one too?" Marlon asked. "Has she been down here? Is that why she is so weird?"

"Not quite," the Shiny said. "Although I do grant you, your mother is an odd one. Your mother received a genetic imprint in order to give birth to you. She is 100 percent human, just a carrier, a carrier of our potential. If you have studied genetics in school you would call it DNA. Margherite was taken and imprinted, not unlike many others on your planet. Her imprinting was designed that she have you, raise you, and in time, you will fulfill the destiny that is a part of you."

MarlonDale noticed that the Shiny's voice deepened and started to sound like the butler, Mr. French, talking to Buffy and Jody from that show he watched on Nickelodeon.

"So I am a shiny, or at least part shiny?" Marlon asked with the first of a thousand questions.

"A Shiny," Mr. French said, again with a grin. "Well, yes, yes you are. Welcome to the home of the 'Shinies' then. My name is," the Shiny paused. "Well, for now, why don't you call me Host, I am your host, so call me Host. I believe there is some symbolism there, yes? Host represents the body of Jesus Christ, if my Comparative Planetary Religions 101 course was accurate.

And, I am your Host to an entire body of knowledge. Knowledge you will find 10 million times more interesting and credible than your Earthly confabulations of heaven, hell, sinners, saints, saviors and redemption. Come with, and we can engage while we walk. Well, we don't actually walk here Marlon, it is more of a flow. The medium is very conducive to ease, so enjoy."

Chapter 33

Marlon and his Host covered a lot of territory spatially and mentally, in what seemed to be a short time span, if time was measurable. They passed a variety of geological liquiform structures. Host answered Marlon's questions of where they were, who they are and what his part in this Mercury Vapor Experience was to be. Host began with something of a tutorial on the Earth's structure. Host wanted Marlon to have a basic understanding of their purpose. He wanted MarlonDale to accept his participation in it as easily as he was able to glide about in their current environment. Effortlessly and without question. " Marlon, the Earth's Crust is like the skin of an apple," Host said. "It is very thin in comparison to the other three layers. And there are two types of the Earth's crust. The crust, under the oceans, aptly named the Oceanic Crust, is only about eight kilometers, three to five miles thick. The Continental Crust, the layer where you earth beings live, is about 32 kilometers, twenty five miles thick. The temperatures of the crust vary from the temperature of the air on top, cold in winter, hot in summer, to about 870 degrees Celsius, 1600 degrees Fahrenheit in the deepest parts of the crust. Marlon, which measurement for temperature are you most familiar, it is Fahrenheit, is it not?

"Yes. Fahrenheit," Marlon answered. He had glided at least 20 feet forward during his two word answer.

"The crust of the Earth is formed by pieces called plates," Host said. "The plates 'float' kind of how we are now. Gentle, flowing. The plates float on a softer, pliable layer which is located below the crust. These plates usually move along smoothly but sometimes they get stuck and a pressure develops between the plates. The pressure builds until,"

Marlon interrupted, "An Earthquake happens. I'm ahead of my class. I read a lot about science and mathematics."

"I know you do Marlon. There's a very good reason you intellectually outpace nearly every one of your 10 year old classmates. We'll come to that in due time." Host said. "Marlon, I hope you are paying close attention to climate changes, and weather events such as earthquakes, hurricanes, tsunamis. There is a reason your planet is talking in these ways." The Host's head shook slowly left and right. "If your species listened to your planet, they would understand. A pity they do not."

Host continued, "The Continental Crust is composed primarily of granite. The Oceanic Crust is basaltic rock. Basaltic rocks of the ocean plates are much denser and heavier than the granite rock of the Continental plates

Because of this, the continents ride on the denser oceanic plates. Ah, and then, below that, below the Oceanic plate, we get down to the next layer, called the Mantle.

The Mantle is the largest layer of the Earth, 1,800 miles thick. The Mantle is composed of very hot, dense rock. This layer of rock is molten, it even flows much like the hot asphalt used for your roadways. This flow, the movement, is due to great temperature differences from the bottom to the top of the Mantle.

The movement of the Mantle is the reason that the plates of the Earth move. It really makes the Mantle layer a very important part in maintaining the stability of your planet. The temperature of the Mantle varies from 1600 degrees Fahrenheit in the uppermost sections of the mantle, to 4000 degrees Fahrenheit near the bottom, nearer the very center of the Earth. The system is set up very much like a Jawbreaker, layered with different characteristics and flavors, but all part of the one.

The very core of Earth, is like a ball of super hot metals all in the liquid state between 4000 and 9000 degrees Fahrenheit. The outer layer of the core is composed of the melted metals, primarily nickel and iron. And Marlon, if we have an outer, we must have an inner, yes?" Host asked. He continued to explain, not giving Marlon the opportunity to answer.

"The inner core of the Earth has temperatures and pressures so great that the metals are squeezed together and are not able to move about like a liquid, but are forced to vibrate in place as a solid. Physics be damned, a liquid acting as a solid, Marlon."

"Kind of like Mercury," Marlon said. "Solid at colder temperatures, liquid at room temperature. We did an experiment with it in science class."

"Yes, very intuitive Marlon. Very good," Host said.

"Thanks," Marlon said.

The Aspie and the Host continued to glide about the city. Shinies scurried about. A busy Monday. The Host continued his lecture.

"The pressure in the inner core is 45,000,000 pounds per square inch, three million times that of the pressure on your front porch," Host said.

"It's surprising that we don't have more Earthquakes, given the pressure difference," Marlon commented.

Host steepled his fingers together and bowed slightly to his guest. "Very good, young man. So, from what I've told you, where in the Earth do you think we are?"

Marlon hesitated briefly, as if time was relevant, and answered, "If we are too far down in the Continental Crust we would melt. So, I think we have to be in the Crust somewhere, but not all that far in."

"Very rational, but incorrect. I'll help you. We are centered in the Mantle," Host explained.

Marlon began to interrupt, but was stopped by a telepathic brake.

"Marlon, when you travel as a result of the properties of the Mercury Vapor Emission, you enter a parallel reality. You no longer have characteristics of a human. You become a, well, a Shiny," Host explained good naturedly.

"But you just said the pressure was three mill," Marlon said. Another telepathic binder was applied.

"Marlon, it is irrational to argue. You can be assured that we are currently in Planet Earth's Mantle layer," Host said.

Marlon felt a hint of aggravation from Host.

"My dear boy, perhaps as you may have postulated, we, me, the other beings you have so eloquently named 'Shinies,' are visitors to this planet. We don't require air, water, or temperate climates. Those are all in a very dissimilar plane of existence than ours."

"Ok. Ok. Then where are you from?" Marlon asked.

"Good question young man. We're from many places. Originally, the constellation Libra, a mere 20 light years away as well as others. Planets not at all like yours. Dissimilar, hazardous, noxious, toxic climates. Not at all what your scientists seem to feel are necessary to support life.

Most of your research seems to base its priorities on water content. A trivial concoction of a couple Hydrogen atoms and an Oxygen. Nothing fantastically original there, but you people are stuck on water. Water this, water that, water content on Mars, rivers on Mars, water on Neptune and water, part of the composition of Saturn's rings. Water, water everywhere and not a drop to drink, I recall was the cry of the Ancient Mariner. Much ado about nothing, yes? Water, so naïve and simplistic."

The Host held his palms out, opened and closed his tendril-like fingers. He opened his palms up. In the center of each hand lay a small sphere of glistening silver, the size of a roulette marble. He held them out to Marlon.

"Now, Mercury, Mercury is the Holy Grail of elemental composition, my good friend Marlon. Mercury," Host said.

Host clapped both hands. Red, yellow and silver sparks shot upwards as if he were holding a Roman candle.

"Whoa," Marlon said as he glided backwards.

"Just making a point with some theatrics. Marlon," Host said. "We will be helping you along on this journey. In time, you will be able to relate this experience to a select few, who will also know. It is only this select few will be able to understand and appreciate what you have experienced. You will intuitively know who you can share with. We'll be in touch."

And with that, Marlon found himself in the back of an ambulance on the way to the hospital for re-warming after a near hypothermic death experience.

Or a dream.

Or the most incredible secret.

Chapter 34

Host was correct. MarlonDale was only able to relate his experience with alternative realities and extraterrestrials to a select few. First was Dr. Sutherland. McAllister Sutherland, ten letters first name, ten letters last name. Just as the Host had explained, he intuitively felt compelled to tell her during that very first counseling session about his contact with aliens. Dr. Sutherland had explained that she was familiar with the endless possibilities that extraterrestrials and parallel universes offer to one's imagination. Dr. Sutherland explained that it is only sensible to accept the fact that differing species from all planets do not necessarily have to reside on the surface or in our time and place.

Why couldn't some take up residence within a planet. MarlonDale agreed wholeheartedly.

He thought he could share with JoHanna Ann Steinburgh, ten letters first name, ten letters last name. And, JoHanna Ann was his best friend, confidant and a fellow Aspie.

So they watched the lamps light, but for quite some time, she didn't see the Shinies. He kept his secret from her. Perhaps it wasn't time for her to know.

Then, when JoHanna witnessed the appearance of the repairmen, MarlonDale was sure she was more like him than she was even aware. Marlon deduced that perhaps other Aspies were the offspring of Shinies just as he was. He wondered about Roberta.

"Maybe I have a larger family than just the Hendershats," Marlon thought.

Chapter 35

During the years in counseling, Dr. Sutherland favored MarlonDale. He received extra time and attention. MarlonDale's neuronal re-programming enhanced his telepathic abilities. It seemed she was in his head all the time. He was being groomed.

It took several years in which Dr. Sutherland weaved MarlonDale's life into hers. She used an assortment of methods to re-program MarlonDale's thought processes. Sometimes he had to solve riddles, form anagrams, find a hidden meaning in a story. He took more than a hundred multiple question behavioral tests, submitted to hypnosis and at times, just sit and listen to incredulous stories Dr. Sutherland told.

Dr. Sutherland explained that she had been abducted by the Shinies when she was 10. She received instruction and ongoing guidance from another being, similar to MarlonDale's Host. Her life had been lived according to a plan she had no part in defining.

"More than thirty years ago, they were still experimenting on humans," Dr. Sutherland explained. "It was frightening and wonderful at the same time. My 'Host' told me the experimentation would leave me sterile. However, he said I would not want to procreate, and that I had a much higher purpose than having children.

"Weren't you sad about that?" Marlon asked.
"No, I was never sad or experienced misgivings.
They rewired that area of my brain, in the same
fashion that I am rewiring yours, so that I would
not have one moment of emotional suffering. A
very loving 'Host,' don't you think?"

"I suppose so," Marlon said, a slight hesitance
in his voice.

"MarlonDale, my purpose, my particular
destiny, was to develop you. Almost like giving
birth you see. You have an important purpose
that so many depend on. You have certain tasks
to complete in order for other events to happen,"
Dr. Sutherland explained.

"Well, what is it that I am supposed to do?"
Marlon asked more than once over the years.

Dr. Sutherland would respond "We'll know
when it is time MarlonDale, we'll know."

At age 20, MarlonDale had yet to be asked to
perform any kind of all-important alien mission.
All that was about to change.

Chapter 36

In a repeat of the previous week's activities, MarlonDale and JoHanna Ann were once again the porch at dusk, waiting. MarlonDale looked over at JoHanna Ann, who was munching popcorn and sipping her Dr. Pepper. She was looking up and down the subdivision street, head bobbing as the lamps lit and the street rolled back.

Two Shinies popped up directly in front of the porch. It startled her and JoHanna Ann dropped her Dr. Pepper. It rolled, spilling the soda between the porch planks. Neither Marlon or JoHanna looked down.

The Shinies motioned for JoHanna and MarlonDale to come off the porch.

"Marlon, I hear them," JoHanna said. "They want us to go down with them. Are you kidding me, we're going down with them?"

"I guess it's your time to know JoHanna Ann Steinburgh?"

"Know? Know what?"

"It has been ten years since I've gone with them," MarlonDale said as he rose.

He took JoHanna Ann's hand and they walked towards the Shinies. The Shinies did an abrupt, Gestapoesque turn, and glided to the roadway. They turned around waiting for

MarlonDale and JoHanna, who had just reached where the curb had been. Another step onto the ground, and swirl, Screaming Eagle roller coaster, down the four of them went.

They arrived in the Mantle and the first thing MarlonDale noticed was how exciting everything felt. During his last visit, a decade earlier, there was a busy feeling, a weekday, a work day, but nothing as energized as it was this day.

Today, the gooey, aqueous environ buzzed with energy. It was Saturday night. The structures were alive and pulsing, much taller than they were in his last visit. The buildings reached out of sight and wavered and shimmied in the gel. There were thousands of Shinies busily Shinying, or whatever it is that they do.

MarlonDale had never been to Times Square, but certainly this is what a galactic, Mantle Layer Times Square, must be like, if there were Time.

Upon recovering from the descent, JoHanna was enjoying the sense of the glide, the ease, weightlessness. Her intellect was attempting to explain the phenomena.

"Marlon and Johanna, welcome," Host said.

"Well, hello to you, it has been a long time," Marlon replied.

"Time, Marlon is not a measured quantity, it just is." Host turned to JoHanna. "Please don't waste your well-developed IQ on using logic to explain your current experience. Like time, it just is. Marlon, you've been brought back for a reason. The two of you have work to do. The 'just is,' 'the time,' is approaching. It is the moon and Desdemona is the sun, your destiny awaits.

Chapter 37

Marlon telepathically spoke to the Host, "Dr. Sutherland explained as much to me."

JoHanna's eyes grew wide as she also heard what Marlon was thinking. Marlon continued, "Dr. Sutherland said that I would do something. She would never elaborate, though. I must have asked her a thousand times to tell me what it is I am supposed to do."

"I am well aware of Dr. Sutherland's counsel to you and to you too, JoHanna," Host said. "That is why you are here together. In fact, there is a third, his name is Alton, but his 'just is' is not ready yet."

"Alton Maliz, from our group?" JoHanna asked.

"Yes, Alton will be joining you on your tasks. He has some rather special abilities," Host said.

Marlon was surprised and concerned. "Alton is a very peculiar guy," Marlon said. "His mind is different, he is into some really strange stuff. Not that, that is necessarily a bad thing for a group like ours. Most everyone who has ever met anyone from our group has said that our brains are pretty different and we are a peculiar bunch

But, Alton has a streak of malevolence and mystery whipped up with his genius and Aspergers. Are you sure? Alton is," Marlon felt the Host's telepathic brake and stopped his Alton rant. "Never mind, I get it, it just is," Marlon said. The Host nodded his gangly head towards them.

"Yes, Marlon, yes," Host said. "Intellectually, the three of you will find the errands you will be going on to be distasteful. I will take the liberty of scrambling your neuronal pathways so you won't have any emotional attachment to the chores."

"Scrambling our neuronal pathways, like Dr. Sutherland has been doing?" Marlon asked. "

"Yes, quite similar," Host replied.

"Can I ask you a question?" JoHanna asked.

"JoHanna, you wonder why is it that we need you." Host replied. "We are an advanced civilization, capable of bending time, traveling through space, adapting and living in an environment that should not sustain any life. Why do we need two junior college students with behavioral challenges to help us? Fair question, JoHanna."

"Shall I answer, Marlon, or would you like to field this one?" Host asked. "After all, she is your best friend in all the crust," Host said, emphasizing "all the crust" with outstretched arms pointing upwards.

"It just is JoHanna, it just is. Maybe they can't make physical contact above the Mantle, I don't know, it just is," Marlon said.

"Well said Marlon," Host said as he steepled his fingers and bowed slightly at the two of them like a Chinaman.

JoHanna reluctantly accepted the explanation to their enigma, "Maybe it just is, but it just is pretty darn weird."

Host continued as they glided along past wavering towers of plasmic mirror. "Now, your first task is to eliminate Edward Relfing , a researcher and professor of Electrical Engineering and Physics, working on the campus of the Monsanto Corporation. Alton will be helpful in this regard."

Marlon scrunched his forehead, his eyes looking up puzzled.

"Eliminate, like kill?" Marlon asked.

Before either Marlon or JoHanna could utter another word, Host held up his hands.

Marlon noticed that the skin of each palm was raised. A shimmering ovoid mass glistened underneath.

"The sprakling marbles of Mercury?" Marlon recalled.

Host placed a palm of each of his hands on their foreheads. JoHanna flinched, her head bobbed once and then remained still as the Host lightly touched her forehead.

Marlon said, "Uh, what, uh."

Host interrupted him. "Please, don't be alarmed with all this talk of elimination killing, death," Host said, pressing lightly against their foreheads.

He continued, "As Kierkegaard said, 'There are, as is known, insects that die in the moment of fertilization. So it is with all joy: life's highest, most splendid moment of enjoyment is accompanied by death.' I'm remapping thought pathways. Neither of you will express any further concern about the elimination, the killing if you will, of Dr. Relfing."

It wasn't as if he had performed a knifeless lobotomy or that Marlon and JoHanna were suddenly exhibiting a flat affect as a result of large doses of Haldol. In their minds, the chore of killing one Edward Relfing was just something that had to be done, to be accomplished with no more or less emotion than flossing one's teeth.

"We'll be in touch," Host said and dissipated in a wave of sparkles.

Instantly back on the porch, JoHanna was reaching for her spilled can of Dr. Pepper. Marlon was holding her other hand. They looked at each other, their eyes met. They exchanged a look of wonder and determination.

Chapter 38

Dr. Edward Relfing, at 39 years of age, had spent his entire adult life working with calculations of energy, matter and space. A child prodigy of sorts, he graduated from the University of Rolla at 19. He attended MIT and had gone on to become a full professor at 26, completing a dissertation on Wormholes, Alchemical and Electrical Energies.

Although he was successful in academia, he also was interested in furthering his research. Beyond that which the academic world would support. He took a researcher's position at Monsanto in St. Louis that was partially funded by a black op governmental agency interested in the applicability of Radionic Theory.

Certain governmental agencies with alphabet acronyms were interested in Radionics due to its promise in mind control, energy field manipulation and healing, applications clearly beneficial to governmental operations.

Dr. Relfing had tinkered with Radionic technology for years. A small circle of people studied and practiced a form of Radionics, in much the same fashion that a few folks studied black magic in the middle ages. Dr. Relfing's colleagues at Monsanto knew his public persona, the eccentric, quiet and distant researcher who worked in a small lab, had no staff and never discussed his work.

His secret life was spent developing advanced Radionics technology that could very well change everything. He shared only some of his findings with his government sponsors. Things like the manipulation of energy fields that interrupted all forms of communication which certainly held promise on the field of battle. Things like the application of transcranial magnetic forces to evoke or resolve migraine type head pain could yield practical application in both the field of medicine and interrogation.

He held close to the vest his development of what he termed, "RIAR" Radionics Initiated Altered Realities, that government dollars sponsored.

Dr. Relfing named his invention the Radionic Portal Challenger. Using the device, he had been able to locate portals and briefly move from the physical to the astral plane of existence discovering a parallel reality. Using his Challenger, he could momentarily flash to the 1880s, a witness to a poker game in Deadwood, South Dakota, to the 1980 fall of the Berlin Wall, or floating in a weightless environ in deep space.

They were brief transfers lasting but a few seconds each trip, before his awareness returned to the lab. However, recently he had made a discovery which would indeed change everything.

An entry from his journal read: *"Quite by accident, I have located a particularly unique location in my lab near my workbench. I recently installed a new overhead Mercury Vapor lamp above the Challenger. The room temperature in the area is 22 degrees Fahrenheit warmer. The temperature increase is confined to a cone shape beginning at the origin of the light. Intuitively I felt I should outline the base of the cone with 20 quartz rocks and crystals. These are part of the samples I've impregnated with the alchemical formulations portal location purposes. I formed a circle on the floor, outlining the edge of the base of the cone. Interestingly, as soon as I placed the last crystal, I noticed sudden weather changes outside my window.*

The clouds suddenly darkened and dust particles sped by the window. I activated my Challenger in the usual fashion. An abrupt and distinct change occurred to the area within the Mercury Vapor cone. Perhaps this is due to some type of an energy quark. The air became wave-like and heavy, aqueous. I was drawn into the cone where I could see figures that may have been human-like, but I could not focus my vision through the thick medium which reminded me of the consistency of blood agar culture plates.

The experience lasted what I think was several minutes, longer than any of my previous portal travels. However, I am not sure at this point exactly how time may function in that plane.

I believe that Mercury is the operative element in this reaction. The Mercury in the lamp is ionized during the lighting initiation, as noted by the immediate and brief, dark blue glow. The ionized Mercury gas pressure increases within the bulb during the lighting process. It is possible that the light produced by Mercury Vapor lamp, in the ultraviolet range was somehow channeled by the Challenger and the crystals to produce a portal. Which allowed me to visualize a concurrent parallel universe. This inter-dimensional door, opened up into different reality, including an astral world. My hypothesis is that this door may be opening to the farthest galaxies in space, a completely alternate reality, or parallel universes on Earth. At this point, I am not sure which is the most likely explanation.

I have repeated this three times now with marvelously consistent results. It is possible that as long as the Mercury Vapor continues generating charges, the portal could remain open. Of course, more research will be conducted at the earliest opportunity. I may introduce additional Mercury Vapor Lamps to increase the size of the portal and the experience."

Dr. Relfing had repeated the same path three times and had stayed for minutes. It was incredibly exciting for Dr. Relfing. He had no idea how accurate his hypothesis concerning an alternate reality "ON" the Earth, or more accurately stated, "IN" the Earth was.

Dr. Relfing was aware of a current train of thought in Radionics, that portals, are controlled by certain inter-dimensional beings that monitor and manipulate those attempting to experience alternate realities. Dr. Relfing was enough of an independent thinker that he questioned whether there were doormen for portals. He had found this one by accident and had returned three times without interference. If there were portal police, he believed he could bypass them.

Apparently, Host was not particularly pleased.

Chapter 39

The fact that the Mercury Vapor Lamp could be the key component in the ability to alter planes of existence with his Challenger was interesting. But what Relfing found most exciting was the fact that he had stumbled upon ET's in the altered reality. And in a consistent , aqueous environment. It was nothing short of remarkable, even for a man like Dr. Relfing.

On the day that the Host notified MarlonDale and JoHanna Ann to whack Dr. Relfing, the scientist was as busy as a blind squirrel trying to find an acorn.

Dr. Relfing was experimenting with the Mercury Vapor ionizing light and its interaction with the Radionics generator.

He theorized that it should be possible to channel the energy from multiple Mercury Vapor Lamps hung in sequence. Along with multiples of alchemical crystals, 40 or 50 and the Challenger, he should be able to travel consistently to whatever reality that the Mercury Vapor produced, and to stay there for prolonged periods of time. Time to explore, take samples, learn. He had not yet perfected the process, experimenting with additional lights, chemicals and crystals.

Like Edison, he felt he had not failed by not finding the correct element for the light bulb, he merely had discovered a thousand filaments that did not work. He would keep experimenting.

Chapter 40

MarlonDale and JoHanna Ann were on their way to group therapy at Dr. Sutherland's. They were apprehensive as to how to approach her with the latest information they received from the Host. Would Dr. Sutherland already know that they had been in contact with Host and that they had gotten an assignment? It seemed likely that she was there to assist them in some way. Perhaps she would give them a gun or poison, or God forbid, a knife.

"I don't know about you Marlon, but I have no desire to stab Dr. Relfing," JoHanna Ann said. "I remember doing pig dissection in anatomy class and almost threw up.
If I threw up on him, it would be disgusting, and I just don't like to throw up. So, if it is a knife, you have to do it. But, if you remember, I have this thing about clean. I do not want bloodstains or mess or spurting arteries. So we have to be tidy about this."

Marlon noticed the increase in the tempo of JoHanna Ann's head bobbing.

"Alright, if it is a knife, I will do it," Marlon said. "But, let's hope we can use something efficient and clean. Weaponry that can be used successfully from a safe distance. Such as a rifle or handgun, something along those lines. I would like to avoid body fluids splashing all about."

It was obvious from the discussion that Host's remapping was a complete success. They discussed freely, and without any hint of compunction, the murder of another human being.

They arrived at Dr. Sutherland's home. After parking the Volvo, they walked onto the porch. Emily opened the door and greeted them as usual.

"Hey guys. How's it going? How are classes?" Emily said, pleasantly engaging in the small talk she had been doing since their childhood.

"It's great Em, I'm taking Calculus this year, it's fun. I hope I will get a good grade this semester," MarlonDale said, hitchhiking his thumb towards JoHanna Ann. "JoHanna Ann gets As, no matter what class it is."

"I got a B+ in my gym class last year. Volleyball was my downfall, if you know what I mean," JoHanna Ann said.

"Tripped and hit the floor too many times?" Emily asked.

JoHanna nodded her head yes as it bobbed down and to the right. She rubbed her knees, always purplish from the continued bruising. .

"Dr. Sutherland is available, just go on in," Emily told them.

They strolled into Dr. Sutherland's office to find her sitting in one of her overstuffed lawyer's chairs, making entries into her journal. She did not pay attention to them for a long minute. When she finally finished writing, she looked up.

"Good afternoon. I understand you may have an interesting experience to talk about. JoHanna took a little trip with you Marlon, is that correct?" Dr. Sutherland asked as she looked over her glasses at JoHanna.

JoHanna Ann and MarlonDale looked at each other briefly as if to ask each other, "How does she know already?"

Marlon spoke in conventional language as the TenSpeak was unnecessary.

"Yes, we both went on a Mercury Vapor Experience and met Host," Marlon said. "I guess we can assume he has been in contact with you."

The conversation turned silent, telepathic.

"Oh, yes, we discussed certain matters and the progression of circumstances and events. Developments are underway as expected and planned. Do you have any questions concerning your, errand, that you were given?" Dr. Sutherland asked.

"We were wondering in what fashion we were to dispose of Dr. Relfing. I have some concerns about how it is to be done, and so does JoHanna," Marlon said.

"Actually, our friend Alton will function as the primary actor in this assignment," Dr. Sutherland said. "As you know from listening to him in group, he has invested a considerable amount of his energy and time building a fantasy world in which he is ruler and almighty over all the Avatars. Which includes the power of life and death. Alton is about as different as they come. I am concerned that he lives a certain portion of his life in this fantasy world that he prefers over our world. His attitude from fantasyland spills over at times and he acts as if he is somewhat of an 'Almighty' in this world. Alton's progress has been challenging.

As you have become aware, I am endowed with certain abilities, relegated to me by the Host, as you call him. This includes clairvoyance, which I frequently channeled in our early counseling sessions. I could tell when one of you, or one of the others, was hiding some aspect of their dysfunction. As you grew older, I did not have to use this power very often. We developed trust and you shared openly. That is not exactly the situation with Alton. I can try to read his thoughts, but at times I am blocked. It makes dealing with Alton, as I say, different and challenging. He is like Forrest Gump's box of chocolates, you never know what you're gonna get." But, he is a good boy overall and the three of you will be quite successful.

Marlon and JoHanna smiled. "Forrest Gump" was one of their favorite movies.

"Nevertheless, Alton will assist you two in the errand," Dr. Sutherland said.

"Dr. Sutherland?" JoHanna said. "Do you think Alton could be violent towards us? I mean, I know he has this imaginary kingdom, we have seen his drawings that he made naming cities, companies and transportation facilities he had taken over.

He had drawings of penal communities too, where the 'disobeyers' as he called them, were systematically tortured. Alton is the poster boy for sadistic tendencies."

Marlon added, "Yes, and he enjoyed speaking of the pain he would cause the 'disobeyers.' He used garrotes and hangmen's nooses, ratcheting chain-driven 'rack'-type devices, electrical shock therapies."

"You needn't worry about Alton acting up against the two of you," Dr. Sutherland said. "His neuronal pathways will be remapped to focus on the task at hand.

Up to now, of course, we have discussed channeling his fantasy into more productive activities, but his knowledge with certain devices will prove helpful in this case. And no, it will not be a knife."

Marlon and JoHanna nodded in the affirmative. JoHanna Ann's head bobbed an extra two nods, down and to the right.

Chapter 41

Alton Milaz, pronounced with a long 'I' and long 'A,' MYLAYS, was not an Aspie. His full name was ten letters long, but that was a matter of coincidence. Alton's mother had not been abducted by aliens and impregnated with genetic material.

Shirley Milaz was an ordinary woman who happened to give birth to an extraordinary child. Extraordinary if one defined extraordinary as really fucked up.

There was no pre-natal alcohol abuse, no illicit drug use, no thimerisol vaccines, no physical, emotional or social abuse in the home to explain how Alton turned out. Alton was just wired differently.

As an infant, Alton exhibited projectile vomiting and his record distance at 39 months, still unchallenged, was 18 feet. Carrots and peas, sailing across the entire great room of the Milaz home, striking a center square of Grandma's quilting rack. Grandma did not appreciate the Olympic feat as much as Alton did when he heard about it later.

As an infant and child he did not sleep but two to three hours each day and he continued to vomit after eating.

Shirley and Dan Milaz took Alton to specialist after specialist searching for the causes of his GI problems and their sleep deprivation. Alton tested normal, with no known pathology.

Then one day at age five, just before entering kindergarten, he stopped chucking up food and started sleeping normally. The Milaz family and their doctors were as puzzled by the sudden change for the better as they were in trying to find an explanation for the etiology of the disorder. Nevertheless, they were relieved. However, the celebration was short-lived.

Alton did not play well with others in the school system. He was either aggressive and hostile, at times physically violent towards other children and teachers. Or he secluded himself, refusing to partake in any of the activities.

Shirley and Dan took Alton to psychologists and testing centers.

They learned that Alton had ADHD, ODD, and a potential tendency towards schizophrenia. At 13, he had begun secretly devising his alternate world, and shared this information while under a psychiatrist's drug-induced hypnosis. He described in detail his plans for torture and murder of all "Disobeyers". Alton was institutionalized for three years.

The psychiatric hospital was very modern and allowed most of the patients' free access to the facility, which included a library, movie theatre, fitness center and cafeteria. Alton had his own room with Internet access and cable television.

During the three years there, Alton earned his high school GED, and completed two semesters of college level courses. He liked to read and study, both secluded activities.

Alton, like JoHanna Ann, had a very high IQ. Unfortunately, he did not have any career plans other than ruler of his own world concomitant with power over life and death.

Studying schizophrenia, psychopathy and ADHD, Alton was able to self-actualize his personality disorders and mental challenges. He understood himself better than the staff at the institution. He practiced scripts in responses to the physicians' and counselors' questions and devised responses that were appropriate for a person on the mend.

Alton convinced the staff that he could be released. He received follow up care as an outpatient.

Released at age sixteen, Shirley Milaz heard about Dr. Sutherland's work with difficult cases. Alton was a difficult case to be sure.

Shirley and Dan drove up to the large Victorian home in November 2006. They explained Alton's history in detail. In addition to the fantasy world, ADHD and schizophrenia, they told Dr. Sutherland about his other aberrant behavior characteristics.

Alton enjoyed taping firecrackers to grasshoppers and watching them explode into little pieces. He exhibited cruel behavior towards neighborhood animals, once tying two of the neighbor's cats to the ski rack of their SUV and watching them drive away to work, unaware that the family cat was going to work with them.

Alton was fascinated with explosives and graduated from Fourth of July pyrotechnics to various advanced devices.

He forged convincing documents indicating that he was a contracting and demolition company and was able to obtain a variety of explosives. One of his favorites was Detasheet.

Detasheet is a green pliable plastic explosive material, thin as paper, often used in letter bombs. A Detasheet the size of a business envelope would seriously injure or kill the person opening the letter.

No mailbox was safe in the Milaz neighborhood. Alton obtained blasting caps and Detcord, a rope-like explosive.

Shirley related to Dr. Sutherland that another neighbor, a dog owner, kept their dog on a long rope in the backyard. The dog barked and the noise disturbed Alton. He taped Detcord to the neighbor's dog collar, ran the charging line to his backyard and blew the dog's head off.

Shirley also related that Alton had been caught setting numerous dumpster fires over the years.

And to fulfill the Yarnell triad, when Alton began sleeping longer periods, he was a bed wetter.

Cruelty to animals, bed-wetting and fire-setting, the unholy triad, has been seen in dysfunctional children for decades.

Shirley and Dan had their hands full with Alton and the juvenile authorities prior to his commitment. They hoped that Dr. Sutherland could somehow intervene in a manner that would stop Alton's progression to a violent psychopathic adult.

Dr. Sutherland accepted Alton as a patient. At the time, she was fully engaged as a member of the Host's staff, and had been made aware that Alton would be a new addition to her patient list.

Chapter 42

Three days after her meeting to discuss the Host's plan for Dr. Relfing with Marlon and JoHanna, Dr. Sutherland arranged a meeting of the group. This group consisted of MarlonDale, JoHanna Ann and Alton. They arrived within five minutes of each other at about 3 p.m.

MarlonDale and JoHanna arrived in the Volvo. Alton rode up a few minutes later on his BMW 850 motorbike. He slid in sideways as he came up the gravel lot, kicking up the small brown rocks, pelting the driver's side of the Volvo. MarlonDale and JoHanna were on the front porch chatting with Emily.

"Hey, Alton, chill out, watch the paint job will ya? It's old, the Vo is the only car I have," MarlonDale said.

Alton stood the bike up on its kickstand and dismounted. Methodically, he took off the full-face helmet, hanging it by the chin strap on the hand grips of the handlebars. He removed his fingerless black leather gloves and put them in his jacket pockets. He took off his red and black leather jacket and laid it over the seat.

He removed a Boston Red Sox baseball hat from his saddle bag and put it on with the bill to the rear. Only then did he respond to MarlonDale.

"Fuck you, Marlon! There are more door dings and paint chipped from parking lots on this car than I could ever do. You chill out! Alton doesn't like getting shit from anyone," Alton said. His conversations included frequent use of third person.

Emily stepped out on the porch to limit the confrontation.

"Why don't you all come in?" Emily said. "Dr. Sutherland just texted me that she is ready."

Alton stepped up on the porch, brushed past MarlonDale and JoHanna, and followed Emily down the wooden paneled hallway into Dr. Sutherland's office.

"Hello Alton, Marlon and JoHanna. I hope you are all well," Dr. Sutherland said.

"Great, glad to be here as always Doc," Alton said sarcastically, plopping heavily in a chair.

"This is going to be much harder than I thought," MarlonDale said in a hushed tone to JoHanna.

Alton stood and faced him squarely. He raised his voice a notch.

"I heard that Marlon," Alton said. "You know, you and JoHanna are no fucking rays of sunshine normality either. That fucking TenSpeak bullshit, your compulsion for everything that has to be in some type of order, like the car has to be parked in exactly the same spot. And Alton thinks that the headbobbing by JoHanna is about as distracting as jock itch."

He turned his attention back to Dr. Sutherland. He sat back in the chair, crossed his legs, and in a soft- spoken, even voice said, "So what are we talking about today, Doc?"

Dr. Sutherland ignored Alton's tirade and his turnabout personality change, turning her attention telepathically to Marlon.

"Marlon, I appreciate the fact that you are concerned," Dr. Sutherland said. "You feel apprehensive about how your errand can be accomplished with Alton. I assure you, all of you, that you will be able to complete this task without too much undue problem or aggravation."

She continued, but this time, verbally, "Alton, we are all together today to discuss a mission. You are an important aspect of this task, Alton. Marlon and JoHanna are also important. It will take the three of you to accomplish our goal. This, and other missions, errands so to speak, require a team concept for success. It just does, it just is."

"Can we just get on with whatever we have come to discuss. I have a test tomorrow and I need to study," JoHanna said, fidgeting in her chair, uncomfortable with her new association with Alton.

"A fucking mission, what is this, the CIA? What a bunch of whack jobs. Alton wants to know what the fuck he is even doing here,"

Alton said.

Dr. Sutherland's coruscating eyes focused on Alton.

"Alton, listen carefully," Dr. Sutherland said. "You are part of this team and you will fulfill the task. And, I guarantee, you are going to enjoy it."

Her gaze returned to all three of them.

"You are to go this weekend, and locate Dr. Edward Relfing. I have a packet of information on him, his picture, home address, phone number, his office location on campus, his lab location. Marlon, you will drive the three of you. Alton, you will devise an explosive device that will kill Dr. Relfing.

I know you are creative enough to come up with an appropriate means to our desired end. You will conduct a burglary of either his home or laboratory to place the device. The explosion needs to appear as an accident, so I think your best opportunity will be the lab. He has been experimenting with a lot of electronic, magnetic and chemical reactions there. An explosion would not be totally unexpected. JoHanna, you are a lookout and it is your job to make sure the boys are successful. I do not want any collateral damage. Dr. Relfing will be our only casualty this mission."

Alton could not wait to take the opportunity to gloat.

"Holy Fuck! Killing a doctor. Finally something fun out of this nursery group," Alton said. "Not a problem. Alton has just the thing."

"I knew you would," Dr. Sutherland said. She handed Marlon a large envelope. "Marlon, here is the packet of information on Dr. Relfing. You will plan the details of the engagement, location time, entry and escape route."

Alton jumped up from his chair. "So, the WobbleHead is the brains of the operation? I don't get a say so in how we get in to do the big bang? I just get to set it. Alton thinks that really blows. I would like some fucking input in the 'errand' more than just an explosive tech."

"Yes, Alton, I recognize your need to be involved in the entire operation to fulfill the fantasy you have been having about killing people. And you will help Marlon with the details," Dr. Sutherland said.

"And what am I? Am I just chicken salad here?" JoHanna Ann complained. "What is this? Is there still a 'good old boys club' even in parallel universes? Are there no Ms. Hosts, or is male dominance a standard across all time-space continuums?"Her head bobbing as she spoke, but with a sly smile, half serious, half kidding.

"JoHanna, I am sorry, but your role is somewhat secondary, albeit important, in this chore.

There will be others where you will take a lead role. Please be patient," Dr. Sutherland said, smoothing potentially hurt feelings. "You all can use this time to meet here and plan for this weekend's activities, or you can prepare elsewhere."

"I was just kidding, Dr. Sutherland," JoHanna Ann said.

"JoHanna, if you have to study, I'll take you home. Alton, you and I can get together later and plan. How about at the Chesterfield Barnes and Nobles at 6? When JoHanna is done, she can meet us. Sound good?" MarlonDale said, sounding like a leader.

"I will go, but not just because you are saying so. I'll meet you there buddy. But you're buying coffee and scones for Alton." Alton sneered and jogged out of the office.

Chapter 43

MarlonDale drove JoHanna Ann home. On the way, they discussed the difficulties in working with Alton. MarlonDale agreed with JoHanna Ann that Alton was a jerk and, of the three of them, the craziest.

"He'll probably blow us up while setting the bomb," JoHanna Ann said, chewing her lip, "Maybe it's an alien conspiracy to involve us in a crime that will lock us up forever because we stumbled onto the Mercury Vapor Experience."

Marlon responded, "I have to agree, it is very confusing to me. Discussing murder of a person without a hint of emotion. And worrying more about our own situation and personal safety."

"If this is the 'just is' of a sophisticated and advanced civilization, it surely is not the most comforting and reassuring experience," JoHanna Ann said. "But we're in it and that is just how it is. Hey, I'll call your cell when I'm ready to be picked up."

MarlonDale dropped her off and drove over to Barnes and Noble.

Mr. Leruq was working the register when MarlonDale entered the store. He came around the counter and caught up with Marlon as he was turning to go to the Starbucks counter.

"Marlon, MarlonDale, how are you?" Mr. Leruq said.

Marlon stopped and turned to face Mr. Leruq.

"Hey, hey, hi Mr. Leruq how goes it with you?"

They shook hands and Mr. Leruq cupped an elbow with one hand, his chin with the other. What Margherite called his Jack Benny position. Mr. Leruq looked over the top of his readers at Marlon. "It's been a couple of weeks hasn't it Marlon? Of course, your mother, she's been in several times, but I have not seen you. You look very well, fit and trim."

"Oh, well, it's been a pretty hectic time for me," Marlon said. "I'm sorry I haven't taken the time to come by. Layton and I will definitely be here next Tuesday night. I understand you're hosting my mom's appliance box impressionistic art.

It will be interesting, but you may want to prepare. It's like if people were coming to a Gallagher show."

"Yes, yes, your mother described the process involved in producing a piece of 'Box Art'," Mr. Leruq said, spreading his arms wide as if carrying a large box. "We have plastic sheathing for the floor. If anyone wants one, I have a bunch of pretty red and green cloth aprons in the back somewhere. Remember, we used them when we did adult watercolor class last spring. Your mom brought you and Layton, remember?"

"You should be alright then unless she suddenly improvises something," Marlon said.

"Yes, I know your mother all too well. That is why I allow her the opportunity to present here. I truly believe she has a great talent, waiting to be discovered. She is a blooming flower, there is no doubt," Mr. Leruq said.

"Blooming something, that is an accurate description of my mother," MarlonDale said. "I'm meeting a friend here, we'll be in the back."

"Ta Ta. See you later," Mr. Leruq said with a wave of his wrist.

Chapter 44

MarlonDale heard the loud pipes of a motorcycle pull into the parking lot. Alton screeched to a stop, leaving a little rubber from the back tire of his BMW on the pavement. "Even when no one's watching he's a complete whack job," Marlon said softly to himself.

Relative to the years in counseling with Dr. Sutherland that he and JoHanna Ann spent, Alton was a newbie to the group. Dr. Sutherland's remapping of the human brain apparently takes a while. Alton wasn't there yet. His sophomore status in counseling didn't make Alton any less an asshole or any more palatable that they were going to have to work with him. "It is what it is", Marlon thought.

Alton found Marlon in the back of the store amidst the reference section. There were four large , orange leather stuffed chairs around a square wooden coffee table.

MarlonDale had blackberry scones and cups of coffee laid out.

"I see you remembered the deal," Alton said.

"Yes, I remembered and I hope you like blackberry ones," Marlon said

Alton sank heavily into one of the chairs, dropping his helmet on the floor. It made a loud thump. A browsing customer looked over. Alton flipped him the bird. The browser replaced the book he was perusing and scurried away like a startled mouse.

Alton gulped some coffee, paying no attention to whether it was too hot. Coffee dribbled down his chin. He wiped it away with his hand, rubbing the coffee into the arm of the chair.

"Listen Marlon, I know you guys don't care too much for me. But, I don't mean to be a prick all of the time. It's just that I have a lot of stuff going on in my head. I can't control some of the stuff I do and say. They say Alton doesn't have any filters. So, that's just the way it is with me.

In group, I am usually acting as if I'm involved with whatever fucking Dr. Sutherland is talking about. She's such a busybody. But, Alton knows you have some weird thing going on with her. You doing her? "

Alton smiled with a wicked grin and winked, but continued without allowing time for Marlon to object to the inference that he was 'doing' Dr. Sutherland.

"But, I do have a grasp on what she is all about," Alton said. "I see that you guys are into some weird shit. The Doc has tried to do some programming my brain, remapping it to where I don't feel the need to blow shit up or kill things or give a shit about the trouble I cause when I do. Alton will have none of that reprogramming bullshit."

Alton smelled the blackberry of the scone. "Mmm, Alton likes."

He took a bite and continued talking while chewing.

"I let Dr. Sutherland believe she is making progress and that I do care, but it is an act, and so far, I don't think she has caught on," Alton said.

"Now, about wasting this guy in Monsanto, same as eating scones to me. I could give two shits. As I'm sure all of you in group know, I am a sociopath, a schizoid. I'm fucking crazy. But Alton is crazy like a fox."

"What do you mean by the weird shit we're into?" Marlon asked.

"You know, in private session, the doctor asks me my impressions of the others in the group and we talked about your fascination with the street lights, water towers, collecting shit," Alton paused to slurp more coffee. "And how JoHanna is obsessed with crop circles, her head bobs up and down like a frigid pigeon and why she can't walk two yards without falling over her own feet.

And I am supposed to understand that you both have Asperger's disorder and I can accept you as you are, and be part of the group that helps you both. And you will be part of the group that helps me too. Isn't that just so sweet? Alton thinks it's a bunch of crap."

"I've been going a long time and it's helped me," Marlon said, sipping the hot coffee.

"Yea, but you probably want to be helped. I like me as I am. But, Marlon, man," Alton said, leaning towards Marlon as if to tell a secret. "I do like your whole Mercury Vapor, alternate universe, alien story. Alton thinks that is some cool bull."

MarlonDale started to talk, but Alton came closer, sitting on the edge of the chair.

"Dr. Sutherland brought me into the fold a few sessions back," Alton said. "She explained how she was a conduit for this parallel universe existing inside the fucking Earth. Weird shit, totally fucking bananas, crazy talk, crazy as anything I heard inside the nuthouse.

But she was serious as a heart attack and I kind of believed it. Alton is wondering whether some of her mind control, programming bullshit is working, or if I believed her because it is true."

MarlonDale sat back in his chair, distancing from the advancing Alton.

"It's been true enough as long as I can remember," MarlonDale said with a deep resolute exhale. "I have been having these visions for years and years. I made contact with them in the Earth's Mantle layer. Someone called the "Host", he's directing the 'errand' to Monsanto. It's very bizarre for sure, but we're in this thing. You, me JoHanna Ann, all integral parts of the machine.

I'm not sure where it is going to end up. Maybe they're planning on taking over the world or something."

Marlon sank deep into the chair, tired of it all for the first time.

Alton sat back in his chair, extended his arms, interlaced his fingers and cracked his knuckles. He folded his hands behind his neck and said, "There's more to your Dr. Sutherland than you even know man. Have you been to the third floor of the house? Alton has, and it is bizarro."

"The one with the knee walls and oval bay windows?" Marlon asked.

"No, the one that has like four columns on the outside where a window should be," Alton answered.

"I have been in every room in that old house," Marlon said. "I don't remember a third floor windowless room, you sure?"

"Absofuckinglutely, Marlon," Alton said. "There is this room, but from the outside there are just columns, third floor. Marlon, think. You must have seen them.

You go up to the third floor and where those columns are, there is this room. A fucking room to somewhere else. You know, Twilight Zone, that show on Nickelodeon. Alton thinks it's some kind of portal. Your kind of place, spaceboy."

Marlon's forehead wrinkled and he shook his head with a healthy degree of skepticism.

"We've been through every inch of that house, inside out," Marlon said.

"Don't I know," Alton said. "JoHanna is like the anal queen of the measuring tape. But, you guys missed it. It's easy to miss. I stumbled across the room by accident one day.

Emily was downstairs. The waiting room was full because Dr. Sutherland was busy with some patient crisis bullshit. The office was running behind. You and blueprint girl were there, but you went outside, walking the grounds. I was exploring the upstairs when I heard, or more like, I felt a buzzing sensation from the end of the third-floor hallway.

I can see how you missed it, Marlon. There's no goddamn door and it is really no more than a good-sized closet. I went to the source of the buzzing and there was this oval wooden block in the middle of the wall. I touched it and it zapped the shit out of me, but instead of the pain you get when you shock yourself, it felt good. Fuck, Marlon, I tell you, it almost felt like I was going to shoot my wad. And then I rotated or dissolved or whatever, into this room. The walls were covered with a shiny liquid. I ran my hand along the wall. It looked wet, but it was dry, just like Mercury from a busted thermometer. And then zap!"

Alton sat up and clapped his hands to emphasize his point. Marlon jerked from the sting of the noise.

"And then I was shifted to what I suspect is your street light world," Alton said. "Alton wants to know what you think of that Aspie boy?"

Marlon pursed his lips and a crease developed over his eyes.

"A portal to the Mantle without Mercury Vapor Light catalyst," Marlon said thinking out loud.

"It felt weird," Alton continued. "The air felt heavier than air, but I could breathe fine. It kind of was like being in water, if you know what I mean. Alton liked it."

Marlon nodded his head. He knew very well. He sat stunned.

"And there were all these silvery beings zipping here and there," Alton said. "Twinkles of light following them as they moved around. And there were really tall structures that seemed to meld into whatever it was that would be the sky. Boy was it warm. Alton had to take off his shirt it was so fucking hot."

Marlon slumped even deeper into his chair. The overstuffed pillows surrounded him, offering him little comfort.

I thought that JoHanna and I were the only ones," Marlon said. "Alton, you were there at the same place we went. Dr. Sutherland, our group, and her house are all connected.

To think that this has all been planned for years. Like we are actors in a play directed by Host."

"Yea. Alton thinks that's pretty fucked up," Alton said.

Marlon picked up his coffee and gulped.

"What else happened when you were in the Mantle layer?" Marlon asked.

"Well, none of the little shiny things paid any attention to me," Alton said. "It was as if I were watching a movie of this strange new world. I was there but not in the sense that I was part of it. I called out to a couple of the little fuckers, but they did not answer. I tried to chase after one of them. But instead of moving I hovered like I was treading water. And then," Alton clapped again, "I was back in the hallway. Alton hasn't told anyone about this until you, now."

MarlonDale's cell rang. He answered and then hung up.

"I'm gonna go pick up JoHanna Ann at her house," Marlon said. "You wanna go along for the ride there with me?"

"Are you fucking crazy, and leave my bike here?" Alton asked. "If someone tried to steal it, Mr. 'Light in the Loafers' wouldn't do shit to stop them, that's for sure. Alton will stay here and save our seats."

Marlon picked up JoHanna Ann. She got in the car and tossed a few books and her art portfolio case in the back seat.

"And what do you have in the case, JoHanna Ann?"

"My stuff from Dr. Sutherland's," JoHanna Ann said. "The blueprints and some notes. For some reason, I just felt I might need them for tonight. So, how is it going with Alton?"

"You are not going to believe what he just said." As he drove, MarlonDale related Alton's story.

"I guess nothing should surprise us now," JoHanna Ann said. "Let me read this to you, Marlon. Tell me if you think this is kind of a weird coincidence that I had this as homework today from lit class."

JoHanna Ann took a square of paper from her pocket and unfolded it. Her head bobbed twice and she cleared her throat.

"From "Shakespeare's 'As You Like It':
All the world's a stage,
And all the men and women merely players;
That's what you and Alton are saying, we're just actors, directed by Dr. Sutherland and the Host.
They have their exits and their entrances,
And one man in his time plays many parts,
His acts being seven ages. At first the infant,
Mewling and puking in the nurse's arms.
Didn't Alton have that vomiting disorder?
Then the whining schoolboy, with his satchel
You first got into this MVE at 10, you probably whined.
And shining morning face,
A reference to shining? The shinies?
Creeping like snail
Unwillingly to school
Don't we all have school troubles?
And then the lover,
Sighing like furnace, with a woeful ballad

A furnace, hot, a Mantle is above a furnace. And killing someone is woeful for the killee.

Made to his mistress' eyebrow.

"We haven't gotten to the mistress part, unless we want to call Dr. Sutherland all of our lovers. I know, it's a stretch.

Then a soldier,

This is where we are now. Soldiers on missions.

Full of strange oaths and bearded like the pard,

I call killing someone a strange oath.

Jealous in honor, sudden and quick in quarrel,
Seeking the bubble reputation
Even in the cannon's mouth.

"The rest is all about getting old, which I hope we will."

JoHanna Ann refolded the paper and put it back in her pocket.

"Makes you wonder whether Shakespeare was one of them, too," Marlon said as he parked.

JoHanna Ann grabbed her portfolio case. "I think the Host quoted Shakespeare a few times. Maybe old Willy Shakespeare was one of them, or us."

They stopped by the Starbucks counter and got three more coffees, returning to Alton who had his legs up on the table.

"What do we have there, your etchings, Pablo?" Alton asked too loud.

"MarlonDale told me about your room discovery," JoHanna said. "Now I know why I had the feeling I should bring this."

She held the portfolio case up with one hand.

"These are detailed sketches of Dr. Sutherland's home, including every measurement of every room on the third floor," JoHanna said. "Let's see if we can find a physical space that is the portal."

Marlon sat down.

"Why would Dr. Sutherland keep the room secret from me?" Marlon asked as JoHanna went through her sketches. "I told her every single thing about the MV Experiences. Ever since I was a kid, I told her everything. I told her about my near death from the hypothermia. I told her about us meeting the Host and everything. Yet, the bitch always had access to the Mantle layer."

Marlon's voice was stained with anger and hurt.

Alton slapped Marlon on the shoulder.

"Right on, MarlonDale," Alton said. "Grow some testicles. You should be pissed off. Alton says fuck Dr. Sutherland and her shining, fucking, secret room, mind control bullcrap!"

Mr. Leruq strolled by and gave a disapproving look at the group as he turned up an aisle out of sight.

"MarlonDale, Alton, keep it down, will you?" JoHanna Ann said with the scolding tone of a school teaching nun.

Marlon grumbled indistinguishable words and sank back into his chair. Alton flipped JoHanna Ann his middle finger.

JoHanna Ann located the third floor blueprint sketch. She measured and re-measured the rooms, comparing them to the exterior dimensions and indeed found a 10-foot-by-10-foot discrepancy.

She noted the four columns on the exterior of the house, in the exact position as the room. She shared her findings with her partners.

"See what I mean?" Alton said. "I wasn't shittin' you. The room is there, a portal to another dimension. An express train that runs all the time. Marlon, you can only hop the train at dusk, and then, on some shiny string bean's street light. Alton says that hot little Dr. Sutherland is the fucking train conductor. That is for sure."

Marlon crossed his arms over his chest and looked down at his feet.

"This is really a lot to digest for one night," Marlon said.

JoHanna drank some coffee and put her feet up on the table. She faced Alton, their new partner in crime.

"Alton, how is it that you ended up here with us, in Dr. Sutherland's care?" JoHanna asked. "You're different than us. I mean, don't get me, don't take this the wrong way. None of us are as disturbed in the violent sense as you are."

Chapter 45

Alton leaned forward and snatched up the rest of Marlon's scone.

"Fair question, JoHanna," Alton said, crumbs tumbling from his mouth as he spoke. "So, you already knew I got sent to this institution for some shit I did. Everyone there is certifiably crazy. It's a nuthouse. I was in for three years. It was a decent place. Cable TV, movies, a library. The food wasn't all that bad either. But it was no prom dance. Alton was drugged pretty heavily for the first year or so. Man, I was still a kid back then."

Alton paused and took a deep breath, letting out some of the past.

"So one day, I am channel surfing in a dope-induced haze, and I start watching the movie "Cuckoos Nest.' Alton says that this is my fucking life story. So here's the test, am I the Chief, Billy, or Randle McMurphy? Who do you think?"

Before either Marlon or JoHanna could answer, Alton answered his own question.

"I was the Big Fuckin Indian Chief, who else?" Alton said. "The Chief played deaf and dumb so he could really hear what was going on in the place. That's what I do. I played along. The place was so idiotic, shit, they even had 'Slingblade' on for a month. The movie 'Slingblade' in the lounge of a nuthouse, with a bunch of nut job kids watching it over and over. 'Slingblade,' about a crazy fucker who killed his mother, her lover and at the end of the flick, he split open Dwight Yoakam's skull with a lawn mower blade. Showing a violent movie to violent nutcases, like me. Alton thought that was pretty stupid.

But I digress. So, I watch 'Cuckoo's Nest' and get the idea to start faking. Fake taking my meds, act half-assed catatonic and start behaving in ways the staff expected me to act. And it worked. They bought my normal act.

I got let out. My mother heard that Dr. Sutherland was doing some pretty good work with disturbed youths like you and she sent me there. I've always known, even before this shiny world crap, I've always known that I was going to be in charge of something big. Something big." Alton stood up and held his arms out in a Jesus pose.

"I will be omnipotent in my world," Alton said. "Dogs and cats beware, blonde girls with freckles and buck teeth, definitely beware. Alton is going to have some fun."

A small drip of spit formed at the corner of Alton's mouth, and dribbled down as he sat. He finished off his coffee.

MarlonDale sensed that Alton had gone somewhere in his mind while talking about the animals and girls. Not a very nice place, he thought.

"Don't get me wrong now, when I say that Dr. Sutherland helped me," Alton said.

"I mean, she is a bitch for keeping you in the dark all those years, but after a month of that intense private counseling with her I started to understand Alton a little better. I understand other people's frame of reference somewhat better. I can emotionally resonate, let's say, how my neighbor felt, when I blew her fucking dog's head off. I can feel that poor Mrs. Schneider was sad and empty after the loss of her pet. I can certainly acknowledge and accept her anger and frustration of living next door to a kid like me. I understand and can relate. I just don't give a shit. Because watching that yappy ass dog's head fly almost fifty feet was about the funniest fucking thing I have ever seen. Alton laughed a lot for days after that and he still gets a chuckle thinking about it." He laughed and shook his head from side to side.

JoHanna Ann was a dog lover and thought his comment was repulsive.

"You really are sicker than even I thought," JoHanna Ann said.

Alton looked directly in her eyes.

"Yes I am," Alton said. "Alton says you ought to be glad I am on your team."

JoHanna Ann felt a shiver from the malignant tone of his voice.

Alton suddenly stood.

"Alton needs another scone," Alton said.

Alton left them. MarlonDale did nothing but shake his head back and forth. JoHanna Ann's head bobbed vertically almost in unison.

Alton returned with three scones and handed them out as if he was a waiter. He gave Marlon and JoHanna napkins as well.

"Thanks, Alton, that's very nice, don't you think so, JoHanna?" Marlon asked.

Alton didn't allow time for JoHanna to respond. He bit off half of his scone and talked with his mouthful again, "So, after I discovered the silver room and now having listened to your stories, I believe that it is more than coincidence that you are all under Sutherland's care," Alton said. "Did you ever wonder why Dr. Sutherland is a whiz with Aspergers and Autism? Alton wondered and found out. I like research. I found that there have been a number of strange occurrences related to Aspergers disorder. Some murders, several disappearances, and anecdotal stories of, get this, alien abduction.

There are just too many references and coincidences having to do with aliens for me. I've come to the conclusion that Dr. Sutherland, you and JoHanna and a couple of the other long-term group patients, all with Aspergers, are maybe, not human beings. You all are either aliens, or, which I think more likely, are all connected in some fashion to beings from another, or a parallel universe. It's the Aspergers or something that's hard wired into your heads that lets all of you find each other, talk to each other, communicate."

Alton spoke like he was delivering an attorney's opening statement. "You both seemed fairly normal, and maybe that's how they are infiltrating us. Using Aspies who are high functioning." Alton said. "Except for that annoying TenSpeak and thigh tapping crap, you seem OK Marlon. But that's your sign to others. And JoHanna, that fucking head bobbing thing is your telltale sign that you are one of them. If you would say cocksucker as you jerked your noggin', I would think you had Tourettes. Don't you get fucking dizzy, for Chrissake? Can't they do a surgery or something to keep your head still. Alton finds it very annoying.

Alton did not stop to wait for either one of them to respond. "Have you ever stopped to consider that I am the only one of the group patients who is not an Aspie?" Alton asked them. "Why do you suppose I am part of the Asperger club?" Alton held his palm up before either Marlon or JoHanna could answer. " I think I'm the Sammy the Bull, the Frank Nitty, the Jose Oquendo. I'm the utility player, the guy who gets things done. I think Sutherland doesn't know for sure whether the brain remapping is solid enough to allow your psyche to kill. I think she's afraid that at the last moment, you'll experience a synapse of conscience and be unable to complete the 'errand.' But Alton, shit. Alton has no conscience. Sutherland is well aware of that. You may very well be the wheel men in this caper, but Alton is the guy going into the bank with the guns. And I am the one who is NOT an alien and part of this conspiracy to do whatever the fuck your silver buddies are planning!"

JoHanna, still fuming about the dog beheading said, "So we are the bad guys! And you are the Earthling who has infiltrated the aliens. You are the 'One' from the Matrix, so to speak? You're going to stop the alien takeover or whatever it is that is going on?" JoHanna Ann folded her hands over her heart and rapidly blinked her eyes. She raised the pitch of her voice to a steely pink falsetto.

"Oh, you're so wonderful Alton," JoHanna said. "And once you've saved the world, you are free to torture beagles and buck-teethed blondes. Another Dennis Rader, Bind, Torture Kill, BTK on the loose? I think I would rather have shiny liquid people around."

"Touché, little lady, touché," Alton said. "OK, OK, I was a little rough on your head bobbing. Alton is sorry. See, see how Dr. Sutherland has me involved in your feelings? Empathic, yea that's it empathic. But, remember my Aspie friend, you are part of the Monsanto assassination team, on the way to send a human to meet his maker. So, Alton says that it wouldn't be wise to get that holier than thou attitude with me."

JoHanna Ann grunted, head bobbing and looked to MarlonDale for support. Marlon just glared at Alton.

Alton continued, "I want no part of the silver world, no hyperthermia, no unscheduled trips inside the Earth. Alton thinks that is bullshit.

So, I sought answers as to how in the hell can I keep Dr. Sutherland and your Host turd, and you, if need be, out of my head. I found the information I needed and using my well above-average intellect, constructed an item of clothing that interfered with the mind control operation and the underworld departures. With my invention, I could go in the third floor room and just be in a Goddamn closet.

And, not only that, when Dr. Sutherland tries to get into my brain to remap it, to tell it to accept this new shiny, subterranean, new world, she is locked the fuck out. You see, Alton could feel her trying to get in his head. And you know what I have to say to that? Fuck that shit.

Alton has his own new world to create, and it does not include molten lava lamp, shiny people. No it does not. And when I wear my invention, Sutherland cannot get into Alton's head."

JoHanna Ann's sarcasm continued. "Does your wondrous invention also let you read minds?" JoHanna asked. "So have you learned the real intentions of the Host? Is the Earth being taken over by silver, alien beings? Are we part of the invasion force, Recon Team 1?"

"The device I wear keeps them out of my head, it does not get me in theirs," Alton said. "I don't know what the fuck the bastards are up to. It just lets me be me, and lets me stay right the fuck here. Whatever your little Mercury people are up to, including Dr. Sutherland, it remains a mystery. Alton thinks they are up to no good."

He gulped down more coffee.

"What do you think Marlon? You're just sitting there letting us bicker." Alton said.

"And I just wish the two of you would quit," Marlon said. Marlon stared at both of them briefly before continuing. "Dr. Sutherland has always said that Aspergers made us unique. Those of us with it belonged to an exclusive group. She made us feel as if we had innate abilities. That we possessed special skill sets, despite our idiosyncratic behaviors. I felt like I was eccentric, instead of a freak. I didn't think it was because I was an alien. I believed neuronal remapping was helping us be more human. Certainly not less, not extraterrestrial, groomed to invade the Earth? But now, the murder we must do, having no feeling? No emotion about killing some guy we don't even know? I know I should feel some hesitation, but I don't. And I know I should because I know it's wrong."

Marlon nodded his head and chewed on his lower lip before he continued.

"Alton is right about her being in my head now," Marlon said. "What about this blocker, your invention, device, whatever it is?"

"Well boys and girls, I'm wearing it now," Alton said tipping his baseball cap off as if showing appreciation to an admiring crowd of fans.

"It's in my BoSox baseball hat. It's just like not taking the meds in the nut house. It fools them. Blocks anyone from opening the door to my head. I've made some improvements to the initial model. The one I am wearing now has a sensor in the head band that sends a slight vibration that lets me know when someone or something is trying to get into my head.

It has yet to give notice when the two of you are around, so I felt it safe to discuss this with you. I'm fairly certain you both are not full fledged members of Reckon 1. At least not yet.

I'm working on a larger scale, a body suit, coveralls. The active material is called VeloStat. Alton knows you are amazed. Trust Alton, it really works."

Chapter 46

Alton narrated a tale that would have enchanted a gaggle of Trekkies at a Star Trek convention. The research he had undertaken had discovered a number of Web sites devoted to alien abduction, impregnation of humans by aliens for the purpose of propagation of the alien species, reptilian aliens, alien intervention as a causative factor in the increased diagnoses of Autism, and how to keep aliens out of one's head using a material made by 3M Manufacturing, called Velostat.

Alton was leaning forward on his elbows. "Velostat is a carbon impregnated, black polyethylene film that comes in sheets or rolls. It is sold in either 4 or 8 miles thicknesses.

"I've just been buying sheets of it, but I may have to purchase rolls if we need volume. It can be heat sealed, taped, glued, sewed. It is not affected by humidity or aging and could be used to line walls or ceilings if need be. The material blocks alien neuroelectric wavelengths from gaining access to the human brain.

I know you both are into math and physics so the basis for the mechanism of action of the hat is much akin to a Faraday cage, but with a few subtle differences. A Faraday cage is a metallic enclosure that prevents the entry or escape of an electromagnetic field. Faraday cages are used in electronic labs where stray electromagnetic fields must be kept out, like during use of wireless receiving equipment."

JoHanna Ann bobbed her head several times down and to the right before turning to MarlonDale.

"We used a Gamry VistaShield Faraday cage in electrochemistry lab," JoHanna said. "Remember the class I had with all the research homework?" She asked Marlon.

MarlonDale started to answer JoHanna Ann, but Alton interrupted in an effort to explain.

"Yea, I've read about Gamrys," Alton said. "Anyway, what makes the Velostat material special is that Faraday cage needs a ground. The Velostat is grounded to the wearer by means of the ionic potential of the skin, our sodium and chloride ions on skin and sweat. Are you with me so far? You starting to believe me now?"

MarlonDale and JoHanna Ann looked at each other, looked back at Alton and in unison nodded their heads, JoHanna Ann more aggressively than MarlonDale.

"Are you familiar with the phenomena of Van Ecks Phreaking?" Alton asked.

MarlonDale sat up as if on a perch.

"It's bizarre, but I wrote a paper on Van Eck," MarlonDale said.

MarlonDale explained that he had to do a biography on a scientist his senior year, and he found William Van Eck's work very stimulating.

Marlon explained that Van Eck was a Dutch computer researcher who devised a method of eavesdropping on computer monitors and other devices that emit electromagnetic waves

In response, and to protect sensitive information, a shielding method was developed to block Van Eck's type of snooping.

MarlonDale told his fellow scone eaters, that Van Eck's technology is in use today in all areas of the private and governmental sectors who desire greater levels of security. MarlonDale explained that after reading about Van Eck, he talked to his father about the whole concept of EMF shielding. His father thought it made sense given the fact that they were doing some groundbreaking research on controlling viruses.

"My dad got a $4 million grant from the government," Marlon said proudly. "They are developing technology to fight pandemics and biological agents."

MarlonDale explained that his father called someone in Washington, D.C., about the shielding issue.

"Some company from out in California, Parabend Technologies, came out," MarlonDale said. "They sprayed the lab with ink, covering all the walls. They sprayed the ceilings, windows, everywhere an EMF could enter. The ink contained a carrier material, probably something like Velostat." Marlon said. Alton nodded his head in agreement. "Dad said it's a continuous conducive layer of metal shielding. When grounded, it protects the lab from all outside EMFs. And it keeps all the EMF from escaping as well. Good enough for the government, it's good enough for us."

MarlonDale was convinced that Alton's hat might actually work.

Chapter 47

Feeling grandiose, like a symphony director, Alton continued his diatribe.

"The both of you suffer from Aspergers Disease Alien Disorder, ADAD, how about that?" Alton said. "You have become so engrained with Sutherland's counseling and the remapping of your brains about the alternate reality that you fail to see the obvious and draw logical conclusions. Let Alton help you connect the dots."

Alton drew imaginary lines between imaginary dots in front of them.

"This thing is about Mercury Vapor Lamps, right?" Alton asked.

Head bobs by MarlonDale and JoHanna.

Alton continued, "Mercury, liquid silver, just like the aliens and the plasmic environment of place down under where we go. Mercury. Mercury implicated in the cause of Autism. Mercury in dental fillings. Mercury is some bad shit. Got it? And that is where these guys are from. Mercury."

MarlonDale interrupted. "Alton, the Host already told us where they were from. Some planet in the Libra constellation many light years away."

Alton stood up and said, "Oh fuck!" and then plopped back into his chair. "Just how retarded are you MarlonDale? You believe whatever anybody tells you? If you believe anything, that any of them said, then you are crazy. And you need to be wearing one of those football helmets those wobbleheaded kids wear, who bang their heads on the floor. And you need to move into one of the padded rooms at my old nuthouse."

"He's got a point." JoHanna Ann said. "I mean about who we believe MarlonDale, not the whole helmet thing. That's just rude Alton."

"OK. OK. OK. Hear me out before you butt in again." Alton said and continued.

"Mercury is the only solid planet other than Earth known to have a magnetic field. That's interesting isn't it? Mercury doesn't have much of an atmosphere because it's so close to the Sun, and in size it's about intermediate between the Earth and its Moon.

Mercury has a high mean density similar to those of the Earth and Venus. Another important similarity. Hmm, similar size, density, magnetic field. But, no atmosphere. But who needs an atmosphere if you don't live on the surface?"

Alton munched on a scone and swigged some coffee down.

"Did you ever stop to wonder that Venus rhymes with penis and we have a planet called Uranus," Alton said, laughing at his own joke.

"Those were some screwy planet-naming Greeks, he said. " But given that Greeks were famous for butt pirating, go figure."

Alton chuckled again at his own joke.

MarlonDale shook his head, JoHanna Ann bobbed. Nevertheless, their attention was focused on what Alton was saying, even his bad jokes. He was making more sense than either of them desired.

Alton moved shifted over to the wooden table and sat on the edge facing them. He was excited at having captivated his fellow hit squad members.

"Earth and Venus are relatively large planets and so have enough overlying mass, their crust layers, to compress their interiors. Kind of like a tootsie roll pop, lots of hard candy on the outside." Alton said.

"This is not so with Mercury. It's more like a whopper. It's density can only be explained by the presence of a greater proportion of heavy elements. Mercury's composition is roughly 70 percent Iron, with a little Nickel, and some Silicate material. The majority of this Iron is believed to be housed in a large core that probably accounts for 75 percent of Mercury's radius. What a core, huh? Like the malted milk stuff in a whopper.

The presence of all this Iron also explains the presence of Mercury's magnetic field. Assume, given what we have recently learned, that the Mercurian's live or lived before coming here, within the Iron, superheated, molted core of their own planet. And let's say for some reason that they need a new home. Maybe their Iron core is disintegrating, changing the magnetic potential which would surely pull their planet out of orbit towards a disaster. You know, like in Superman where Krypton blew up. Instead of just sending only one Clark Kent, the whole population or a bunch of the little shiny bastards escaped."

Alton paused. As if he were Johnny Olson announcing on 'The Price is Right,' he said, "Mercurian people, Come On Down!"

"So, the Mercurians came here and took up residence inside Earth," Alton said. "And why not? The Earth's core is superheated, plasmic. Just like home to the shiny suckers. Maybe the tall buildings are condos. Maybe the Mercurians are selling Earth Mantel Time shares, who the fuck knows? The question is, what part do we play in this drama? And Alton wants to know what is so important about killing this Dr. Relfing?"

Chapter 48

MarlonDale and JoHanna Ann were immersed in thought, trying to rapidly absorb the possibilities. The quiet was terrifyingly loud. JoHanna's head bobbed every other heartbeat. MarlonDale reached over and grabbed her hand.

"JoHanna Ann, are you, are you going to be alright?" MarlonDale asked.

"Yea, yea," JoHanna said. "It's fucking overhwhelming. Me, you, Alton, aliens and Mercurians. It is so much to process all at one time."

She barked her comments in frustration and took a deep breath, consciously slowing her head bobbing to its normal rate.

"Holy shit. JoHanna Ann said a bad word," Alton said in a fourth grader tone.

"You were doing good Alton, don't be an ass now," MarlonDale said. "This is a lot to absorb in a short time."

"Yea, OK. I propose that we go to my house, make both of you hats, and see how you think and feel with those babies on," Alton said. "We can easily test this hypothesis by wearing them tomorrow at dusk and waiting for the street lights to come on."

MarlonDale and JoHanna agreed. They followed Alton to his house. A couple hours later, JoHanna Ann was sporting a St. Louis Cardinals cap and MarlonDale a Chicago Cubs hat.

Chapter 49

There were three chairs on the front porch of MarlonDale's home. JoHanna Ann had made popcorn and each of them had a bowl and a Dr. Pepper.

Alton fidgeted as they waited.

"What are you going to do if you don't see the street fold back?" Alton asked. "Kind of life changing, don't you think? Alton wants to know if Marlon is going to freak out?"

Alton began singing a version of the Cops TV show theme song, "Bad Boys, Bad Boys, what you gonna do, what you gonna do when they DON'T come for you. Bad Boys, Bad Boys, what you gonna do, what you gonna do Marlon, if they DON'T come for you?"

"What if they don't come, and there is no MVE?" MarlonDale said. "Alton, I've thought about that a lot since last night. It's bizarre enough thinking that I am maternally, genetically Mercurian. But to discover I'm being manipulated by aliens, for what? And lied to by Dr. Sutherland for the past decade. If so, what the hell am I supposed to do?"

Marlon was exasperated.

"I say we go find out what this Dr. Relfing at Monsanto is doing," Alton said. "If the shiny spacemen want him offed, either he could be an ally to us, or he is really one dangerous motherfucker. Alton says we go visit him prepared for either eventuality."

"I slept with my ball cap on all last night," JoHanna said. "I was hoping it would erase this remapping about killing. It must not have worked. I still know we have to do it and if we do, it just is. I just sound so blasé' about killing someone, it's so weird."

"Yea, I did the same thing last night, too, JoHanna," Marlon said. "Completing our 'errand' seems like turning in homework on time."

"Maybe it doesn't work on damage already done," Alton said. "Alton will research that next. So, when do the street lights come on?"

With the question posed, the street light in front of MarlonDale's house began to flicker. The charging was taking place, the Mercury vapor excited. The lamps up and down the street emitted a steady white stream.

MarlonDale and JoHanna Ann held their breaths. Alton took a long draw on his Dr. Pepper. After one minute, nothing happened. A neighbor backed out of the driveway and drove up the street. Two minutes, nothing. Three. Five minutes, no change.

Marlon stood and kicked his lawn chair across the porch.

"Son of a bitch, the fucking thing really does work!" MarlonDale yelled, uncharacteristically loud and profane.

'Yes, my two afflicted Aspergerian partners in crime and punishment," Alton said.

"Introducing to you, the 'Alton Milaz Velostat Electromagnetic Force Alien Blocking Hat.' "

Alton took a bow, one arm behind his back.

"All of your thoughts that once were, are no longer," Alton said. "All of that which was done, will now be undone."Alton said philosophically, using MarlonDale's TenSpeak.

Marlon reached his hand out and shook Alton's.

"MarlonDale says yes, we certainly have work to do." MarlonDale said in Alton's third person speak.

Chapter 50

It grew darker on Marlon's street. The repairmen did not appear.

The three formulated a plan. First, because the darkness provided cover, they decided to do some reconnaissance on Dr. Relfing. They surveilled his home, a small bungalow in Kirkwood.

There were no lights on, no cars in the driveway, the door on the unattached garage was closed, and leaves were piled up in front of it as if it had been undisturbed for several days. It did not appear that Dr. Relfing was home. During their second drive by, JoHanna noted that the mailbox on the porch was overstuffed. Maybe Relfing was on vacation.

They parked the Volvo a block away and walked towards the house, three young adults wearing ball caps, looking as if they were on their way to a sporting event or the mall. JoHanna Ann maintained watch from a closed service station lot across the street, with her phone in hand ready to notify MarlonDale immediately of any problem.

Alton and MarlonDale cut through a neighbor's yard and hopped the three-foot chain link fence surrounding Dr. Relfing's back yard.

The yard was unkempt, not surprisingly for someone of Relfing's background. Researchers generally find no time for mundane necessary activities and leave those to the less gifted.

In Terry Hendershat's case, the less gifted usually were Layton and MarlonDale.

There were no lights visible from the rear of the home. Alton noted that there was a sliding glass door. Alton gave MarlonDale a pair of brown jersey gloves.

"We don't want to leave any evidence that we were here," Alton said as he pulled on the gloves."We can get in through the slider, piece of cake."

They walked onto the back porch. Alton checked to see if the slider was unlocked, but it was locked. He told Marlon to check the back door and garage doors.

"No sense in breaking in, if Relfing left a door unlocked," Alton whispered.

All the doors were locked. They checked above doors, under potted plants for an extra key, but found none.

"Shit, I guess this guy just wants us to break in," Alton said. "I think I can get the slider without much trouble. Take this screwdriver and do what I do."

Together they pried up the bottom of the sliding glass door. There was enough play at the top of the door that by prying up the door from the bottom, they were able to lift the entire bottom edge of the door over the track. They pulled the bottom of the door out a few inches and away from the top track, removing the entire door from the frame. They leaned it against the side of the house.

"Easy as can be," Alton said. "I used to do this all the time in my neighborhood. I'd eat a little something from a neighbor's fridge, take a crap or piss on the kitchen floor. Put the door back in place and wait for them to come home. Sometimes they would call the cops. It was great theatre of the absurd."

Chapter 51

Alton and MarlonDale entered the house. MarlonDale texted JoHanna and told her they were in. She remained vigilant at her post. They searched the house. Unlike the exterior, the inside of the house was immaculate and orderly. After a few minutes of noticing the degree at which Dr. Relfing kept his things arranged, MarlonDale concluded that Relfing was OCD, and perhaps an Aspie. Dr. Relfing's bookshelves were arranged by genre, alphabetically by author, and by size. The complete collections of Isaac Asimov, Gene Roddenberry, Roger Zelazny, Scott Wittenburg and Michio Kaku, gurus of parallel universe theory.
Texts by Albert Einstein, Stephen Hawkings, and Thomas Edison, were shelved. Clean, dusted, orderly.

The kitchen cabinets were stocked according to nutritional value, proteins, carbohydrates and fats - saturated versus unsaturated. Everything was labeled and stored in neatly-arranged Tupperware containers.

French doors led to Dr. Relfing's study. The doors were open. The room focused to the far corner where four computers and servers were blinking, acknowledging their entry. Alton and MarlonDale immediately noticed that the windows and walls were covered with black plastic sheathing. Velostat.

Alton flicked the mouse on each of the computers to see if any were currently performing activities. They defaulted to a nondescript screen saver, with a window asking for a password.

They rifled through desk drawers finding nothing of interest. The file cabinets were locked, which Alton easily picked.

There were folders and files categorized by activity and date, reaching back to Relfing's high school years. They conducted a thorough search, finding nothing of particularly relevant material.

"Look here, Marlon," Alton said as he opened the last of the six file cabinets. "The top two drawers are full like all the others, the third drawer is half full, and the fourth drawer is full. That's odd, don't you think, as organized as he is? Why wouldn't the third drawer be full and the last drawer waiting to be filled up?"

"That is very odd, I would never file so haphazardly," MarlonDale said. "My guess is those files were removed for a reason." He peered into the file cabinet. "The wire bar in the third drawer is way back."

"Yea. That drawer was full, no question," Alton said as he pulled a few folders out from the first two drawers and read the labeled tabs.

"Relfing is very much into EMF and Chi, some really esoteric, heady integrative medicine healing concepts. There are files on Channeling, Reiki, Radionics. Alton says this guy was way out there."

Alton replaced the files and took a few out of the third drawer.

"These are basically notes and programs from what looks like his experiments last year and up until two months ago," Alton said.

Alton bent down and reached into the fourth drawer and retrieved several large spiral bound log books. He opened them up on the desk.

"These are experiments and journal entries from, looks like, all last year," Alton said. "I don't know. Maybe he keeps only some of his stuff at home and the rest at his lab. Is it hot as hell in here or what? His furnace must be set on 90. Let's move on."

MarlonDale's phone chirped. JoHanna Ann texted that the same car had driven around the block twice now.

"He's not here. Let's go to Monsanto," Alton said.

Chapter 52

During the 25-minute drive to the Monsanto campus, the trio discussed their next move. Alton indicated that Monsanto may not be as easy to access as Relfing's home. There were gates and security guards. Fortunately, the building housing Dr. Relfing's laboratory was at the far south end of the campus, fairly secluded from main drives. A guard would really have to be serious about his job to check this area more than once per shift. Alton devised a plan to park in a subdivision about three blocks from the south end of the campus and walk in. They would cut a section of the chain-link fence behind Relfing's building, which was identified as "RD Twelve".

They would get in the building to find his office, Room 3C1. Alton brought a backpack containing bolt cutters, timers, rope, duct tape, explosives, and a Glock 9mm pistol.

Alton took out a notepad and re-read the plan:
1. Get in the building.
2. Catch Relfing by surprise, at gunpoint (if he is there). Put a Velostat hat on him.
3. Tie him up to a chair.
4. Tie up and gag witnesses (if any).
5. Interrogate him about everything he knows concerning Mercurians, the Mantle, the Host, Dr. Sutherland.

6. Get him to join their team or....
7. Kill him.

Alton gave JoHanna Ann brown jersey gloves. He pulled three black balaclavas from the backpack.

"Pull these over your face when we get near the building," Alton said. "I hope it's not as hot in there as it was at Relfing's house. These things are toasty."

Alton took the Glock out of the backpack and chambered a round. Marlon and JoHanna winced at the sound the pistol made.

"Hey, hopefully we won't need to use it," Alton said. "But if we do, I need to be ready. Alton always says it is better to have and not need, than need and not have."

Alton put the gun in his waistband.

He cut a small hole through the chain link and they slipped through, climbing over landscaping bushes and gravel walkways. Building RD Twelve, a 3-story, brown brick building was just ahead. There were no cars in any parking spaces around the building.

MarlonDale thought it ironic that the parking lots and the building were illuminated by his old friends, the Silverliners. A few lights inside the building were still on.

Alton used his "EZ Snap" lock picking gun to open the rear door to the building. It took several tries as the spring-loaded pick unscrambled the tumblers. Finally the lock gave way and turned. They went inside.

The hallways were dimly lit by the red EXIT sign. They had entered on the ground level and promptly took the stairwell, figuring that 3C1 was on the third floor.

The third door along the third floor hallway was labeled C1. They peeked inside through the cross-wired, door glass. It was dark and looked as if no one was there. They found it surprising that the door was not locked.

As they entered, Alton used an infrared flashlight. The infrared provided enough light to see, but was invisible to anyone looking from the outside of the building. They noted a typical laboratory setting.

"Looks a lot like the labs at my Dad's place," MarlonDale whispered.

The lab was three long rooms separated by a door. They had moved to C2, finding essentially the same furnishings, computers, desks, files, dry erase boards. At the left of the C3 door was a nameplate for Edward Relfing, PhD.

The door was locked, but quickly succumbed to the "EZ Snap." Alton opened the door and shined the infrared light around. To the rear of C3 lab was another door. A dim light shone through the crack at the bottom of the door.

Using hand gestures similar to those that SWAT Teams employ, Alton silently motioned for Marlon to come with him and for JoHanna to stand guard at the door.

JoHanna Ann glared at Alton and whispered.

"I have to stand watch again? When can I come in and look around?" JoHanna asked.

"I promise on the next killing assignment, you'll be on point," Alton said as he stepped past her, pulling the Glock from his waistband.

There were no windows to peek through. They stood by the door and listened to their hearts beating. Nothing else could be heard. The door opened outwards. Alton positioned himself to the left and motioned for Marlon to turn the doorknob and if it was unlocked, pull the door open.

Marlon opened the door. Alton swung in with the Glock extended from his right arm. They met no resistance upon entry. They saw no one in the room.

It remained quiet and still. Alton relaxed his arm and let the pistol hang down against his thigh.

"Man, it is hotter than hell in here, too. What is it with Relfing and heat?" Alton whispered and answered his own query. "Alton doesn't like it."

They walked further in the room, accessing a far corner where a desk light provided a dim glow. A few yards behind the desk they noted a long, black workshop-style countertop. Above the countertop hung a series of Mercury Vapor lamps, flickering.

Slumped over the desk, in a high back chair, they found Dr. Edward Relfing.

His face was twisted to the right, cheek squished into the keyboard of his laptop. His face was red as a fire truck. Marlon checked for a carotid pulse. No pulse, no respirations, Relfing's skin was extremely warm.

Alton moved Relfing's limp hand off the mouse. It was hot as a toaster. His computer was on, and active. He had been journaling. They lifted him out of the chair.

It was like carrying a hot water bottle. The impact of Relfing's head with the keyboard had entered a series of numbers and letters. After deleting them, they read the last entry:

"This past journey to the Mantle was very disturbing. It seems that my presence was detected. The moment I entered the plasmic medium, the beings scurried into the structures leaving the area, once quite active, rather silent. I quickly redialed the Challenger to return. The temperature in the lab is much too hot. Something has clearly changed. It is well known that parallel universes can leak into each other. Perhaps I have produced a leak.

I must get a thermometer and quantify the temperature in here. It is rapidly rising."

The journal was dated with today's date and timed four hours ago. It ended there.

Alton and MarlonDale noted that everything in the room was extremely warm to the touch.

Not hot enough to brown or burn, but probably 140 degrees. Whatever Relfing had done had taken his life.

MarlonDale and Alton met JoHanna Ann at the doorway and explained what they found. They agreed the best course of action was to get out of there. Alton said he forgot his flashlight in Relfing's office and went to get it. He joined them a minute later and they retraced their steps out of the building.

Hurriedly walking back to the car, they were quiet. Each involved with their own appraisal of the situation and what to do next, but each sharing the same thoughts. An explosion from behind tore through the silence. They looked back to see an orange glow.

Alton smiled.

Chapter 53

The trio met at Barnes and Noble's at 10 a.m. the following morning to develop a plan. Each had watched the morning news. The lead story on all the local channels concerned the explosion on the Monsanto campus and the unfortunate death of Dr. Edward Relfing. Each anchor ended his story with "An investigation is being conducted by local police."

MarlonDale and JoHanna Ann purchased lattes and sat in the café waiting for Alton. MarlonDale had initially thought the explosion was overkill and nothing more than Alton stroking his own ego.

However, after discussion with JoHanna and a decent night's sleep, wearing the ball cap, he realized that destruction of any evidence of portal access to the Mercurians living below was necessary. They were sure that Alton got off on it just the same.

Alton arrived, parking his motorcycle in the parking spot directly in front of the table where they were sitting. He cranked the throttle wide several times and peered in the window to make sure they saw him. He went through the same ritual of helmet, gloves, jacket, ballcap, and entered the store, ordered a coffee and pulled up a chair.

"Pretty exciting stuff. Dead researcher, a huge explosion, an investigation being conducted. Don't you think?" Alton said with a tone of satisfaction. A job well done.

"Yea, really great Alton. I just hope there weren't any cameras that saw us," JoHanna Ann said.

"Hey, we were dressed like Ninjas," Alton said. "But, don't worry about it. I put a medium-sized EMF pulsar in with the explosives. This is new military technology I got a hold of. When the explosion happened, an EMF pulse was generated that blinked all wireless communications, and would damage all receiving equipment of any messages sent within a 3-mile radius.

Any monitoring images from any camera on the Monsanto campus would be scrambled on the receiving end. Plus, we got bigger fish to fry. We are dealing with an onslaught of Mercurian Invaders and you are worrying about local cops. For someone so smart, you sure can be dull as shit. Priorities JoHanna. Get with the program."

"Oh, Alton, you are so, so smart, you really rock," JoHanna Ann said sarcastically.

"Enough already, the both of you need to stop it. The three of us are in this together right now. Let's work as a team and figure this out, OK?" MarlonDale said.

"Right, right, right, uh, sorry JoHanna. Marlon is right," Alton said. "Alton will try to be less of a dickhead. But being considerate runs against Alton's nature."

"OK, then, I will try not being a bitch, too," JoHanna said. "Maybe that runs against my nature too, but I'll try."

Three teenagers wearing baseball caps, sitting in the café at the Chesterfield Barnes and Noble at 10 a.m., devised a plan to save the world from what they thought was an impending takeover by the Mercurians.

Much of the tactical planning was Alton's doing. They would conduct an interrogation of Dr. Sutherland. She was a key player. Her home was a portal to the Mantle. She had consistent communication with the Host and she was a facilitator of the errands.

By 1 p.m., they were pulling into Dr. Sutherland's driveway in Marlon's Volvo, each wearing their ball cap and carrying a backpack of supplies needed for the mission.

As they stepped onto the porch, Emily came out to greet them.

"Hey guys, I didn't think you had an appointment today," Emily said.

"We had a couple of urgent issues that came up. We need to talk to Dr. Sutherland, is she available?" MarlonDale asked.

"Come on in, I think she's doing some reading. There aren't any patients this afternoon until after 3, so you're fine," Emily said.

Emily text messaged Dr. Sutherland, who immediately came out of her office.

"Oh, hello MarlonDale, JoHanna, Alton, please do come on in," Dr. Sutherland said brusquely. They all entered her office. Alton shut the door behind him.

"I see that your first errand was quite successfully completed. There is another chore that you will have to accomplish. This one will be..."Dr. Sutherland said before being interrupted by Alton.

"Enough of your bullshit, doc," Alton said as he pulled a pistol out of his waistband and pointed the business end at Dr. Sutherland.

"As I was saying," Dr. Sutherland continued, unphased by Alton's threat, "this one will be unfortunate, difficult. For you especially MarlonDale it will be hard to understand. I will need to remap all of you right away." Dr. Sutherland spoke with an urgent tone.

Looking directly at MarlonDale, she said, "The Host has deemed it necessary to remove your father. I'm sorry, but Dr. Terry Hendershatt must be eliminated next."

She exhaled deeply, "I really am very, very sorry about this one Marlon."

"Alton does not find that acceptable, doc," Alton said as he fired the weapon, striking Dr. Sutherland in the chest.

The voltage from the Taser darts knocked her to the ground. In choreographed fashion, JoHanna Ann removed a Chicago White Sox cap from her book bag and placed it on Dr. Sutherland's head. She secured it with the chin strap option, as Alton had suggested.

Alton and MarlonDale lifted her to her chair. MarlonDale took the duct tape from his back pack and wrapped Dr. Sutherland's upper torso to the chair. He taped her legs to the feet of the chair. Dr. Sutherland regained motor control suddenly. She jerked several times, pulling her wrists up, wriggling to lean forward away from the chair. The duct tape held her tight and bit into her wrists as she struggled.

"What do you think you are going to do now? Do you not understand what we have worked to accomplish?" Dr. Sutherland asked.

She grimaced with a puzzled and painful look.

"Yea doc, we do understand and pretty damn soon you will, too," Alton said. "Just let the ball cap do its job for a few minutes. You may have some questions pop into that pretty little head of yours, as THEIR ability to get into it weakens. Alton's hat will block that mind control bullshit," He said as he toyed with the Taser.

"And I can tell you for sure, doc, you will answer our questions or you have a world of pain coming your way," Alton said with a menacing and hopeful gleam. "You are going to tell us all about the Mercurians, the Host, the little shiny bastards living in the Mantle layer. All of it."

Alton pulled the trigger on the Taser a second time, giving Dr. Sutherland another jolt for the fun of it.

"Stop it, Alton you'll probably hurt her and we need her," JoHanna Ann said, reaching towards Alton, trying to grab the Taser.

Alton gracefully dodged JoHanna's hands, stepping to the side of Dr. Sutherland.

"OK," JoHanna said. "Alton was just having fun, giving a little payback."

Chapter 54

A few minutes later, Dr. Sutherland regained her senses. "MarlonDale, JoHanna Ann get me loose from this chair immediately." She demanded, as if Marlon were a child.

"Emily, Emily come in here," she bellowed.

A murmur came from behind and to her left. She looked over and saw Emily duct-taped to a chair with a gag in her mouth.

"Emily was a little too noisy for my liking, doc," Alton said. "Now, you are going to be totally honest with us from this point on and tell us exactly what the fuck is going on. Of all people, you know me, my capabilities and desires very well. You know how I will savor everything I do to you. And you will tell us."

"What, what, just what is this about killing my dad?" MarlonDale asked. "What kind of world do you want to live in? The one where the kids are killers, killing their parents? We are with Alton on this one, give it up."

"JoHanna Ann, are you going to allow this to happen?" Dr. Sutherland asked, trying to reason with what she thought was her last hope.

"You want us to kill MarlonDale's father! Fuck you, you crazy bitch," JoHanna Ann said, smiling over at Alton, her head bobbing.

"I see we have a consensus here, doc," Alton said. "So, how about doing some explaining."

Dr. Sutherland sat upright in the chair. She shook her head, her platinum hair flowed over her eyes and covered her face. Her torso quivered, like a wet dog shaking off water. She closed her eyes and leaned her head back, exhaling a deep, raspy breath.

It had been about 15 minutes since JoHanna Ann strapped the Velostat ball cap on the doctor's head.

"I, I feel, odd, I'm not sure what it is. It feels like an unraveling, an unleveling of my mind?" Dr. Sutherland said, rolling her head around several times.

"It's not an un-leveling, doc, it's a clearing out," Alton said.

JoHanna Ann reached over and moved the hair out of Dr. Sutherland's face.

"Alton's invention, the hat you have on, blocks the EMF from the Mercurians," JoHanna said. "It allows you to think freely without interference from them. Please, Dr. Sutherland, tell us what is happening to us."

"The Mercurians, you've figured out the Mercurians and the Host?" She asked.

"I put it all together, once I found that room upstairs, and made the hats," Alton said.

"It's all been about aliens, this whole time Dr. Sutherland?" MarlonDale asked his words bracketed with hurt and anger.

Dr. Sutherland focused intently on each of her patient's faces. Her eyes scanned from Alton to JoHanna and then MarlonDale, where her gaze lingered the longest. She closed her eyes and took in a deep breath. When she opened them, she stared at the floor. Her voice was determined, but laced with a melancholy tone.

"I'm going to tell you all a rather unbelievable story. But, it is true. As you can tell, TenSpeak will no longer be necessary.

Over 100 years ago, the planet Mercury began experiencing an unstable orbit," Dr. Sutherland said. "As you may have assumed, the Mercurians lived within their planet, in the inner iron core. Similar to how we have treated our planet, they bastardized their resources, something akin to mining. Removing some of the iron core, exporting to other galaxies for what we would label as profit. Before any of the Mercurian race knew, enough Iron had been removed to alter the magnetism, pulling them ever so slightly out of orbit. The orbital change produced fluctuations in the density and pressure inside the Mercurian core. These variations slowly made a number of regions within their core unable to sustain life. They realized the need to move some segments of their population to another location. Earth's Mantle layer was similar enough that they came here.

For many, many years, Mercurians have been residing within our planet, without much interference. Their species can survive on the surface of the earth, but they find it, well, they find it uncomfortable. The Mercury Vapor Lamps, the street lights, allow a select few of them to come up and engage in certain human activities to assure stability of this planet. Human activities such as mingling. Or experimenting on our species, or abducting some of us. And the like. So, essentially, until recently, we have been co-existing with them.

Unfortunately, Dr. Edward Relfing discovered a means to access the parallel alien reality in the Mantle layer, and was thus a threat to the status quo of the Earthbound Mercurians. Relfing wasn't the first to stumble onto us. There have been isolated cases like this in a number of countries over the years where someone had to be removed, as it were. The killing, it was all part of it."

Dr. Sutherland's chin trembled and she started to weep. She only allowed herself a few moments of anguish. She sniffed loudly and tried to raise her shoulder to wipe her tears off her cheek. The duct tape was too tight. Marlon took one of his gloves and wiped her face.

"Thank you, Marlon," Dr. Sutherland said. "You've always been such a good boy. You know, there are others like you, like JoHanna, who are allowed to know. Others in China, Africa, Australia, all with varying degrees of Aspergers. Aspergers, the doorway, so to speak."

Dr. Sutherland paused and looked upwards at the bill of the baseball cap. "Quite ingenious, I must admit, Alton," she said. "The normal human brain is primordial, uncivilized, savage in comparison to the polished sophistication of a Mercurial organic intellect. Those of us with Aspergers, and a few of the other Autism Spectrum Disorders, have neuronal pathways that are a refined mosaic of connections, an amalgamation of cortical and limbic architecture, the result of previous extraterrestrial intervention. Over the years, the Mercurians experimented with the human brain and inserted organic behaviors we've come to diagnose as Pervasive Developmental Disorders, including Aspergers. They instilled Aspies with a select number of highly developed neuronal circuits similar to the Mercurian cortex, allowing communication between the species. My mother was one of the thousands of women taken by the Mercurians. And I was taken as well. Some of the experiments they performed resulted in unwanted violent Asperger behavior, such as the killings you hear about on the news now and then, but for the most part, we Aspies are a peaceful and valuable lot."

"Enough with the history and psychology lesson, doc. What is going on?" Alton asked impatiently, pointing the Taser at her.

"I'm getting to that, Alton," Dr. Sutherland said. "Please don't shock me anymore."

"Then get to the fucking point of it all already," Alton said

"In order to solve the problem of the Dr. Relfings of the world, those extraordinarily intuitive humans. Those extremely bright people who, through their own intellect, stumble upon the alternate universe in the Mantle," Dr. Sutherland began, "Well, the Mercurians needed a representative, an intermediary, an agent, to take care of issues above the crust. That's where people like the three of you and me, have come into play over the years."

"Except we're not agents, we're cold-blooded killers for them," MarlonDale interjected.

"Hmm," Dr. Sutherland said, noting the tone and content of MarlonDale's words. "I suppose whatever contraption you have on our heads has essentially undone the remapping of emotion and conscience required for the, errands if you consider yourselves cold blooded killers."

"Congratulations Alton, very clever, deviously so. So very, very much like you. I must admit. I guess I shouldn't be surprised."

"Continue with the story, we are what, for the Mercurians?" Marlon asked.

"We can communicate and thus are called upon to assist from time to time. Yes, there are instances where planned eliminations had to take place to keep a balance," Dr. Sutherland explained.

"But it has not all been violence. A number of our greatest thinkers have been the result of extraterrestrial influence. Franklin, Edison, Ford, Sagan, Hawkings, all influenced by Mercurians."

"Why me, why us, why now, who is the Host?" Marlon sputtered staccatic questions with a mixture of anger and desperation.

"The Host is much like an inter-galactical curator," Dr. Sutherland said. "I think of him as an eternal plate spinner, always juggling, moving, attempting to keep harmony and stasis amidst the universe. Earth is housing about six and one half billion humans and a decent number of Mercurians. And to be fair, we humans have not been very good stewards. Unwisely using the resources of the Earth. We left the harmonious rural environment during the Industrial age, moving to cities, using fossil fuels and depleting natural resources.

Our technology has improved life on the Earth and increased life expectancy, which increased the numbers of inhabitants above the crust. Our lifestyle and our civilization is out of balance with the world. The tectonic plates shift more often, resulting in increased numbers of Earthquakes. A number of volcanoes have become active. Remember Mount Saint Helens? And how about Mount Vesuvius becoming active again? All these stressors increase risk to the stability of the planet, risking not only us, but the Mercurians."

"What does my Dad have to do with this then?" MarlonDale asked.

"I don't know if you were aware, but your father and I were a couple at one time," Dr. Sutherland said.

"No one told me anything about you and my Dad," Marlon said.

"It was well before you were even a thought," Dr. Sutherland continued. "We were in med school at the time. I was taken, programmed, wired, pre-destined, whatever you care to call it. I was supposed to marry your father and have his children. In essence, I was to be your mother." She shivered, her shoulders and head shaking momentarily as if a freezing blast of air had swept through her.

"My, this is unlike anything I've experienced," Dr. Sutherland said. "Even what I'm saying sounds so bizarre, when I hear myself saying it. This device on my head is amazing. I have clarity of presence, but a dissonance from the reality I have perceived my entire life. Quite disturbing and invigorating at the same time." Dr. Sutherland shook her head again, clearing cobwebs.

"Anyway, as Mrs. Terry Hendershat, I was to steer my husband towards certain career paths that would enable us, as a couple, to assist the Host in maintaining balance," Dr. Sutherland continued. "Alton, could you please cut me loose. I am cooperating and this tape is very uncomfortable. I am not an adversary."

"Keep telling your story, doc," Alton said. "Alton will be the judge of whether you are a friendly or not."

"Very well," Dr. Sutherland said. "Missouri is such a critical state. Its centricity to the United States is one important factor in monitoring planetary influences. But more importantly, the New Madrid fault is a significant geological concern to the Mercurians. The Host's plan was that Terry and I would settle in southeast Missouri, near the Bootheel. Your father would have changed his focus in college from medicine to engineering. Terry would work in Geo- Biological research, developing an implantable biologic material that would mend and fuse plate faults.

It was all so elementary. He was to develop a Geo-Bio substance that would grow rapidly in any medium, any environment. It would meld and consolidate dissimilar materials into a single extremely stable and strong solid. Deep drilling would be done to inject the substance into weakened or shifting plate locations, essentially preventing Earthquakes. It would have had utility in volcanic eruptions as well. The end result was to have been a long-term maintenance of the integrity of the Earth's layers, saving the planet from disaster. Or so Terry was to think. It really allowed the Mercurians the ability to control the location and severity of any earthquakes or volcanoes. They could therefore selectively destroy locales anywhere on the planet, or mend them. However, your father met Margherite and she stole him from me, the proverbial snake in the Garden of Eden. And the Geo-Bio project was never undertaken. The stability of the earth is still not under anyone's control, not ours, not the Mercurians."

MarlonDale paced. He was furiously thigh tapping. The tapping had returned as the baseball cap unwired Dr. Sutherland's influence. He stood in front of his former doctor and confidant.

"That does not explain why Host wants my father dead," MarlonDale said.

"Your father's genius would not be denied MarlonDale. He went on to become a well respected researcher. Your father's work in infectious disease has been very prolific," Dr. Sutherland said. "The Host has taken note. As you know, he has developed an anti-viral agent that has the potential for saving millions of lives. That is the quandary. That is the quandary."

Dr. Sutherland started to sob, her words coming in choppy waves.

"I'm so sorry, Marlon. I'm so sorry," Dr. Sutherland said. "I wish it were not so. But the Host. The Host has decreed this be done."

Alton quickly interposed, standing shoulder to shoulder with MarlonDale directly in front of Dr. Sutherland. He looked directly down at Dr. Sutherland with a poker face, unconcerned whether Sutherland was crying or sorry.

"You're dodging doc. What we're doing has nothing to do with tectonic plates and earthquakes. Alton is tiring of this future-past lives, save the planet bullshit," Alton said. "Alton wants an explanation why you wanted us to kill Marlon's dad. I'm getting ready to send a bunch of voltage your way unless you tell us what the fuck this is all about!"

Marlon spoke softly and asked "Why is it a quandary if he can save lives?"

Chapter 55

Dr. Sutherland composed herself. She blinked tears away, returning her gaze to Marlon.

"Because the Geo-Bio project was never undertaken , the Host put into place redundancy plans to assure the stability of this planet and survival of his people." Dr. Sutherland said.

"What plans doc, get to the point!" Alton said.

"Plans to limit the damage the human race has, and is doing. He feels it best if the population is thinned. It was going to be accomplished by targeted earthquake, floods and Tsunamis with application of Terry's GeoBio material . Instead, a cyclical pandemic is on the horizon. A pandemic is the Host's Plan B.

The last major flu pandemic was in 1918. There were 40 million people who died worldwide at that time, some estimates were closer to 100 million. And that was a time when the virus traveled at a snail's pace by train. A new strain of influenza will mutate very soon. More than three million will die in the U.S. alone. Our economy will implode, 10 times worse than it did after 9/11. The worldwide economy will totally crash. There will be hundreds of millions of deaths worldwide. The world is unable to respond to a pandemic.

We will see adversarial nations cooperating to a degree never before seen. Literally, the lion will lay down with the lamb for more than a generation. As the U.S. economy collapses, the nation undergoes a forced change. We revert to a less technologically reliant, less fossil fuel depleting, less polluting, less gluttonous nation. We become more of an Agrarian and Aquarian community."

The corners of her mouth turned up in a slight smile from a long forgotten memory.

"A utopia, MarlonDale," Dr. Sutherland said. "Remember, 'Big Rock Candy Mountain'? How you loved that song, MarlonDale? You were too young to even understand the words, but you loved that song about a wonderful, utopian world." Her smile faded and her gaze shifted to each of her three captors again.

"As a result of the pandemic and the worldwide changes, the Host buys time for the planet, and someone to develop the next Geo-Bio project or whatever the Host wants for his purposes," Dr. Sutherland said. "Perhaps another generation or two will go by before an incarnation of Albert Einstein, Tim Berners-Lee or Bill Gates arrives on the scene to devise whatever technology the 22nd century will bring."

"Fascinating, so fascinating, and terrifying," JoHanna Ann said. "So you know how and when the virus will make the genetic re-assortment to become a pandemic flu?"

"I am so impressed, JoHanna Ann, you are so bright, you will make a superb scientist," Dr. Sutherland said, winking. "Yes, JoHanna, privy to the Host has certain perks. He allows a few clairvoyant encounters to happen, a few prophetic moments to enter my awareness now and then. Yes, you will be quite a gifted scientist."

JoHanna smiled, but her concern about the pandemic returned. "A pandemic is one of the worst disasters Dr. Sutherland. So much disease, so many deaths. Mass graves, mass cremations. I don't even want to think about it."

"I'm sorry, but the current flu, whether it is the H5N1 or the H1N1, will make the genetic leap in Europe, more specifically on a farm in Italy, very soon. The re-assortment of the virus will take place as a bird or swine virus and a human virus engage in a deadly dance within their host, a simple Italian farm pig. The pig will infect the Italian farm family with this new, novel viral strain that can spread easily from person to person. The rest is accomplished by air travel, shipping and the Internet. The World Health Organization, the CDC and a variety of the other worldwide institutions designed to protect our public health will be activated. They will garner a small measure of success in isolating and containing the virus to Europe. We will have a moment of respite in late summer. But, only briefly, very briefly. This new virus is a killing machine, more pestilent than any biblical plagues. It will change the face of the planet, for the better."

Dr. Sutherland noticed Alton's patience waning. His arms were crossed over his chest, the Taser held over his left shoulder, the Taser lines dangling from the gun to her chest like kite string. His finger was stroking the trigger which would deliver another jolt.

"I'm getting to the point, really. Please hear me out completely," Dr. Sutherland said.

Alton's arms uncrossed, his finger cleared from left the trigger.

"MarlonDale, your father's Virotic Vaccine will be called upon at this time of great need," she said. "The world will have reached WHO Pandemic Level Five in which human to human spread of the flu was localized to Europe. We will approach Level Six, where there is an increased and sustained transmission of the virus in the general population worldwide. Millions in Europe will have already died, and the virus will creep into the U.S. from the coasts. The FDA and CDC will authorize immediate and mandatory vaccination with Terry's Virotic to every person in the United States. Other governments across the globe make the same proclamation and the pandemic is stopped before reaping the havoc I mentioned. The pandemic virus promulgated by the Host, while killing people, was designed to heal the planet. Without the pandemic, we don't return to the simpler, more Earth-friendly civilization. Without the pandemic, we hasten the demise of our own species, but even more important to the Host, we continue to decrease the stability of our planet. The Mercurians will not allow that to happen. You cannot fathom how dreadful it feels telling you this. I have never, ever felt a moment of apprehension or dissent from my destined path. Never, until now. This device on my head is quite powerful. I feel emancipated somehow. Autonomous, and at the same time I am sick with guilt and shame on so many levels."

Chapter 56

The three of them stood silent, processing what Dr. Sutherland said. Alton broke the silence.

"I'm having some trouble in buying into your reasoning. You're double-talking us. Preaching pre-destination, the all powerful Host. But so far, everything you say was supposed to happen got fucked up. You didn't marry Marlon's dad. We didn't kill Relfing, he was already dead. We definitely are NOT going to kill Marlon's dad. And as long as I keep that fucking hat on your head, your communication with the Host or any of the other shiny fuckers is out of order."

"You didn't kill Relfing?" Dr. Sutherland asked quizzically.

"He was face down dead when we got there. I threw in the fireworks for free," Alton said.

"Was it hot in the room where you found him, really hot?" she asked.

"Like Hell it was. Probably 120 degrees or better," Alton answered.

"Oh, my Lord, cut me loose. Cut me loose!" Dr. Sutherland screamed, straining at the duct tape.

The three of them were surprised by her volume and tone.

"Whoa. The doctor is coming around. Alton like," Alton said.

"Please understand! As I mentioned, the Host always has redundancy plans," Dr. Sutherland said. "He probably used another trio to kill Relfing. Three who would have performed as instructed. They would have been a parallel Marlon, JoHanna and Alton. Developed for the task when Host learned Alton was using a blocking hat."

"Huh?" Alton muttered.

"Oh yes, eventually he must have figured out your device and your intention. He would have made copies of you three. Replacements that are not human, but quickly cloned products of your DNA. Puppets, Avatars, whatever you wish to call them. There must have been some urgency on his part. Perhaps the virus is readying for the leap. My God. The Host would have had to directly transfer your parallel universe replacements from a reference in the Mantle," Dr. Sutherland said. "They would have come directly from the Mantle to Relfing's, thus the residual heat in their wake. If the heat had not dissipated, you were just behind them."

JoHanna Ann was the first to get it.

"Oh my God, remember the car that went around twice?" JoHanna said.

"At Relfing's house, sure, so?" Alton said.

"I thought something looked very familiar as it went by," JoHanna said. "I think it was Marlon's car that went by then. That was us, leaving Relfing's house, going to the lab. I mean not us, but the other parallel lives us?"

JoHanna Ann wondered if it sounded as weird to them.

"Holy crap. It WAS hotter than hell at Relfings," Alton said. "Alton thinks Dr. Sutherland may not be so full of shit after all."

Dr. Sutherland continued, "That would indicate that your father is in grave danger from the three of you who are not wearing baseball caps." Dr. Sutherland felt worry and apprehension, feelings she had not experienced in 30 years.

"So if I see it right," Alton said, "our options are to kill Marlon's dad, or our replacements kill him. A shitload of people die from the flu, but, we save the planet? He shook his head and waved the Taser around before he continued, "Or, we save Dr. Hendershat and we destroy the planet? What kind of bullshit choices are those? Neither one of those options are acceptable. Dr. Sutherland. You've been in this shit from the beginning. What the fuck do we do?" Alton's tone was somewhere between demanding and pleading.

"The Host holds the key to the problem. We can reach him by going upstairs," Dr. Sutherland said.

Alton abruptly cut her off.

"Fuck that. Fuck that upstairs portal," Alton said. "That fucking room got me involved in this bullshit in the first place," he said. " We go up there, the Host locates us, sends some Avatars, it gets really heated up, and we are snuffed out by the non-hat wearing us. Alton finds that unacceptable, doc."

Alton fingered the Taser trigger.

"Alton, we have to work this thing out together somehow," JoHanna Ann said, trying to convince herself, and all of them, while she simultaneously pushed down Alton's arm holding the Taser.

"I don't know. I'm confused. The Host seems to know everything that occurs or will occur," Dr. Sutherland said and started questioning everything. "Has he always known? My losing Terry to Margherite, did he know that too? Is it all part of his plan? Was it Terry's choice of infectious disease rather than Geobiology? Why? I, I don't know, I am not sure. These hats. They bring doubt and suppositions, confusion, lack of clarity. Or perhaps, perhaps more clarity.
I just can't say for sure, I don't know if these caps block the Host or if he knows what we are doing now."

Chapter 57

Marlon made the command decision to untie Emily and Dr. Sutherland and bring them both with them. Whether or not their options were acceptable, whether or not the Host knew what they were doing, did not alter the fact that three Non-Velostat cap wearing clones were probably on the way to kill his father. He had to do something.

Dr. Sutherland grabbed her doctor's bag and they piled into the Volvo and headed for the Hendershats' residence. On the way, MarlonDale encouraged them to brainstorm for an answer, to just blurt anything out, stream of consciousness ideas.

"We could hide your dad so they can't find him," JoHanna Ann hollered.

"Hiding, great idea, JoHanna, hiding away from our expected locations," MarlonDale added.

"I got it. Marlon, does your mom still have some of those refrigerator boxes?" Alton asked.

"Yea, I think there are two, three in the garage," MarlonDale said.

"We get your dad in the box, we wrap the box with Velostat sheeting, they can't find him," Alton said. "We take him somewhere, somewhere away from here, to give us some time to work this out, to come up with a plan."

"Forget everything I said about you, I love you, man," MarlonDale said, smiling for the first time in several days.

Upon arrival at the Hendershat home, they were disappointed to find no one was t here. But, there were two empty, 6-foot tall, hot water heater boxes in the garage.

MarlonDale called his father's lab and got voice mail. He called his dad's cell phone and got voice mail. He called his mother's cell and got voice mail. He left the same urgent message on each one.

"This is MarlonDale, this is a real emergency, call NOW. I need you to call my cell phone right NOW," MarlonDale said.

A couple minutes later his cell phone rang. It was Margherite.

"What is it Marlon?" Margherite asked. "What is the emergency? I'm at B and N getting ready to do a reading."

MarlonDale explained that he needed to get a hold of his dad, that it was urgent, a matter of life and death. Margherite sensed the drama in her son's voice, but tempered her motherly concern with her selfish histrionics.

"Oh my God, Marlon, what are we to do?" Margherite said. "The gravity of life and death. Does the very existence of the planet depend on finding your father right this moment?"

Her prophetic comments were laced with more sarcasm than Marlon could tolerate.

"YOU ARE FUCKING ONE HUNDRED PERCENT CORRECT MOM, YOU HAPPY?" MarlonDale yelled.

"MarlonDale, do not take that tone with me, I am your mother. Your father is here with me for once, he's actually taking the time to attend one of my readings. Imagine that. And don't think for a minute I am not going to tell him about your attitude."

"Mom, do you see me, JoHanna or Alton anywhere around?" he asked.

"MarlonDale, are you? What is wrong with you?" Margherite said. "Stop being foolish. If you're here at B and N, hang up, you're using your minutes unwisely."

"Mom, we are all wearing baseball caps, wearing baseball caps," MarlonDale instructed. "If you see us without ball caps, hide from us. I know it makes no sense, but just do it."

"Of course, honey, we'll hide, it'll be fun," Margherite said. "Remember when you and Layton used to hide on the bookshelves and under the cash registers, when you were both so little? Mr. Leruq let you have the run of the place. If only you could be little again and…"

MarlonDale hung up the phone realizing how stupid he must have sounded to his mother. What else could she think except that her son had gone from Aspergers to a paranoid delusional?

The group packed a water heater box in the car and drove to Barnes and Noble. Alton busied himself in the back of the Volvo with the box, covering it with the Velostat sheeting from his backpack. Once again proving that duct tape works for anything.

Arriving at the bookstore, they looked in through the windows and did not see their capless selves, or the Hendershats. Going inside, the temperature in the store felt normal. Plan B had not arrived yet.

Alton, MarlonDale and JoHanna Ann ran down the aisle like the Mod Squad, a good 10 yards in front of the ambling Emily and Dr. Sutherland. They made it to the rear of the store, near the artist's presentation room.

There was no additional heat. Seated in stuffed chairs were Mr. And Mrs. Hendershat, silently turning pages in coffee table books, blissfully unaware of the inexplicable turn their lives were about to take.

"Mom, Dad, no time to explain, come with us now," MarlonDale commanded, out of breath.

"What, what's this all about Marlon?" Terry asked, looking up, as if his name had just been called for a haircut.

"No time, both of you, get up now, right now," MarlonDale said loudly.

He was vigorously thigh tapping like a snare drum, the snapping on his jeans nearly as loud as his voice.

Terry stood up.

"Tell me what this is all about," Terry said as the Taser darts hit his chest.

Margherite screamed as Alton removed a hand held stun gun from his jacket pocket and jolted her in the shoulder. Mr. and Mrs. Hendershat crumpled to floor as if slipping on banana peels.

"Marlon, bring your car around back, hurry," Alton said.

As well as any fireman, Alton carried Terry out the back door of the store. JoHanna, Dr. Sutherland and Emily dragged Margherite by the arms out of the store. They all hurried past the bewildered Mr. Leruq, who stood in his usual Jack Benny posture, cupping one elbow with his hand and his chin with the other.

He followed them through the employees-only area towards the back door.

Mr. LeRuq watched as Terry was shoved head first into the water heater box in the back of the Volvo. Margherite was pulled in lying next to the box on her back.

Marlon yelled to Mr. Leruq, "It's my Mom's theatre of the absurd, don't you know?"

Mr. Leruq smiled as the Volvo sped away east on Highway 40.

Chapter 58

As MarlonDale drove, his father and mother regained their senses. Alton continued to place layer upon layer of Velostat and duct tape over the box. It was a cumbersome task in the confined space, straddling the box, or kneeling on Margherite. Terry began yelling and Margherite started shaking, spitting and biting at Alton, as if she were performing.

"Terry, Terry, this is Mac," Dr. Sutherland said loudly towards the box. "Margherite, look at me. Margherite, stop it, stop snipping at Alton. Margherite, look at me."

Margherite's gaze shifted to Dr. Sutherland and she partially composed herself, combing her hair back with her hands. Terry continued to holler from inside the box.

"Terry, can you hear me? It's Mac," she said.

"Mac, Jesus Christ. Yes, yes I can hear you, get me out of here. Marlon what are you doing? What the hell are you people doing? Have you all gone crazy?" Terry asked.

Before answering Terry's legitimate question, Dr. Sutherland directed Marlon.

"MarlonDale, drive to Cahokia Mounds," the doctor said. "Do you know where it is, how to get there?"

"No, I've, I've been there before, I just don't remember," he said.

"No worry, Doc, I've got a Garmin 770. I'll get

us there," Alton said, taking the street navigator GPS device from his backpack and programming it for Marlon.

"Terry, I am sorry you are in the box, but please let me explain," Dr. Sutherland said.

"What kind of explanation can there be for being shocked and kidnapped by my son and his friends and his God damn doctor? This is crazy, let me out of here. You all have a lot of explaining to do!" Terry hollered, and started kicking the end of the box.

Alton had left the Taser barbs in Terry's clothing, feeding the lead wires through the top of the box, sealing the small opening with extra layers of Velostat and duct tape.

A quick pull on the trigger delivered another jolt to Terry. He screamed and went silent again.

Alton smiled. "We can't have you screwing up all of my hard work there Dr. Hendershatt. And Alton likes using the Taser."

"Alton, do not Taser anyone anymore. Let me take care of this, please," Dr. Sutherland pleaded.

"Alright. But, if he starts to get out of the box, I will have to zap him again," Alton said.

Terry was moaning but becoming alert again. "Dammit, stop with the Taser, it hurts like hell."

"Terry, it's Mac. Please listen to me carefully and lie still while I talk. Margherite is right here and is relatively calm, you need to be as well.

"OK, OK, no more shocks," Terry begged.

"Very good," Dr. Sutherland began with calm, controlled speech. "The story I am going to tell you will sound incredulous. I am being candid, straightforward and more honest with you than I have been with anyone in the past 20-plus years. Please hear me out, do not interrupt until I have finished. Agreed?"

"I am about out of free will right now Mac, don't you think? Yes, yes I will shut up and listen," Terry said.

"Margherite, do you understand? Please listen closely and know that I am speaking from my heart with nothing but the best of intentions for you and your family," Dr. Sutherland said as she stroked Margherite's shoulder.

"Yes, of course, Dr. Sutherland," Margherite said.

McAllister Sutherland (ten letters first name, ten letters last name) began her incredibly unbelievable explanation with the alien abduction of her own mother, the Aspergers connection, the counseling sessions, the Host, and continued to the Tasering and stuffing of Terry in the Velostat and duct tape-covered water heater box.

The first to respond was Margherite. "So, in this story, I am the original sin?" she asked. "Had I not met Terry, the world would not be in the mess it is now and we would not be hunted by a trio of parallel universe killers? It's all my fault?"

The tears and rib-grabbing sobs came forth from Margherite like a sudden thunderstorm.

Dr. Sutherland leaned over the back seat to give a two-arm hug to Margherite and assured her.

"Margherite, just as in Eden, we cannot go back, we can only go forward," Dr. Sutherland said. "Please stay with us and help us, stop crying and be with your husband and son, we have much to do."

A few moments later, Margherite stopped sobbing and only sniffled. Alton handed her a blue bandana from the MacGyver backpack.

Chapter 59

As they neared the Cahokia Mounds exit, Dr. Sutherland continued.

"We are going to use the Cahokia Mounds because they are unique and powerful," Dr. Sutherland said. "There are similarities to our situation there, that may be of assistance. Cahokia means 'City of the Sun,' how is that for our first congruence? I think we will be able to play our best poker hand there."

She continued with a calming influence as she spoke.

"Around 720AD, the Cahokian tribes were in danger of being wiped out due to famine and disease," Dr. Sutherland said.

"They had ceased to live with the land, and had turned away from the great nature they were once a part of. Sound vaguely similar to our current situation? Just as large numbers of their people began to die, they were visited by beings from the sky. These beings offered them the knowledge and technology to save their civilization from extinction. These extraterrestrials assured them that the Cahokians would prosper and become one of the most powerful civilizations in the world.

The aliens were not altogether altruistic. The Cahokians had to agree to certain terms in exchange for the assurance that their tribe would flourish. The beings told the Cahokians that in 500 years, they would return to the region, at which time they would collect their payment for the assistance. The Cahokians would have to give the aliens all of the wealth and riches, and all children under the age of 16. The Cahokians accepted these terms and used the knowledge and tools, provided by the aliens, to build the most progressive and advanced civilization in the world. The terms of the pact were forgotten or relegated to folklore. However, on the eve of the 500th anniversary, as the story goes, the ground began to shake and the sky rained fire. There were earthquakes and volcanic eruptions. Another coincidence? I think not. Hundreds of aliens appeared from the sky on the outskirts of the city. Of course, the Cahokians refused to give up their children, or their riches, and began battling the aliens. The Cahokians were no match for the advanced weapons and technology possessed by the beings from another world. They knew their only hope was to turn to a super weapon their forefathers had spoken of in stories passed on from generation to generation. A weapon that was from the 'Great Spirit.' The entire Cahokian population gathered on top of the mounds that they had built as towers to their Gods.

The spiritual leaders and all the citizens of Cahokia focused their psychic energy against the alien attackers. Using their minds, they projected thoughts of doom against the beings. Psychic energy built up in the mounds. The ground began to shake violently. As the alien attack force approached the city, the mounds let loose a powerful psychic oscillating wave that emanated out from the city in all directions. An electromagnetic force expanding at a rate of thousands of feet per second. Do you see the comparison? EMF then, EMF now. The psychic pulse was so overwhelming that it killed all of the alien attackers. Sometimes the cure kills the disease, but unfortunately also kills the patient. The pulse wave annihilated nearly the entire Cahokian civilization as well. Buildings crumbled to dust from the psychic energy force. All that remains are the mounds."

Dr. Sutherland continued speaking. Everyone in the car was spellbound. The only other discernable sound was the tires rolling on gravel roads leading to the mounds.

"We must use the only power we have to reckon, or reason, with the Host," Dr. Sutherland said. "We have our combined energies, the EMF protection of the Velostat and our intellect. We'll go to the largest mound, Monks Mound, and make our petition."

Chapter 60

Marlon parked the Volvo and everyone got out. Alton and JoHanna fashioned scarves out of the Velostat sheet for Emily and Margherite for their protection. Alton cut the bottom of the box to allow Terry's feet to emerge. They agreed that because Terry was the target, he needed full body protection. The six of them trudged up to the top of Monks Mound, helping the tall box waddle his way up.

They reached the top of the mound and found the approximate center.

"Alton, I need that can of spray paint in your backpack," Dr. Sutherland said.

With a puzzled look on his face, Alton handed her a can of purple spray paint from his backpack. She outlined a circle 10 feet in diameter. She took an aluminum bottle from her bag and poured a viscous silvery, metallic fluid along the purple circle. She removed a handful of crystals from her bag, and placed them at the ten, two and four position Marlon noticed the positioning, and thought of saying something about Dr. Pepper, but decided otherwise.

"Make a circle around Terry, join hands," Dr. Sutherland instructed the group. "I want you all to find a high C note and hum it. All together, we must pray. Pray to God for an answer. Pray that he will spare the life of a good man, Terry Hendershat, that he will spare our planet from destruction by Earthquake and fire, pray that he will save humanity from the coming pandemic. Pray together. Focus as the Cahokians must have. Feel the energy from our souls merging. Pray, hum, pray, hum, pray."

As they prayed and hummed, the quartz crystals flickered, in much the same fashion as a Silverliner when coming to life. Suddenly, a coruscating luminescence of light and sparks radiated upwards to the sky from the circle of silvery fluid and the crystals.

MarlonDale thought it reminded him of the beams of white light that shone up into the sky at the site of World Trade Center that one year.

Their circle was totally immersed in white light, brighter than a thousand King Kong search lights. Only the boxed Terry was not temporarily blinded. The others fell to their knees, covering their eyes, their humming turned to howling, in fear.

MarlonDale screamed, "Dad, Dad the light is so bright, so painfully bright!"

"Marlon, Marlon, where are you?" Terry yelled.

"Here I am, here, here I am, I am here," MarlonDale answered.

Terry threw the box off and crawled to his son. He called out to the others and they all came, all kneeling, shuddering, cringing, clinging to each other, huddling together.

As suddenly as the light appeared it dimmed, the crystals glowed a steady 40-watt fluorescent level. The Host spoke to them telepathically.

"You have called me. You are asking for things you know not. McAllister, you know the most, but you know little. Things are. They must be. It just is," Host said.

"Please, please, Father, there must be a way to save the life of this good man, this good and decent man that I have loved for my entire life?" Dr. Sutherland begged.

"The way is written, it shall not be unwritten," the Host said. "The Mercurians are my chosen people. They turned from me on their home planet, as many on this planet have turned away. I have a bond, a covenant with Mercury, the planet closest to the Sun, I always have and always will."

MarlonDale pushed himself to his feet, reaching up, shaking his left fist, while thigh tapping with the right.

"You kill my father and millions will die on Earth. Please, that makes no sense to me, not at all. Whoever you are, Host, God would not be so cruel!" MarlonDale said.

"Many things I have done are thought to be malicious and heartless, these things just are by necessity," Host said. "We cannot easily change what has to be, young MarlonDale. The only answer is to alter the past. If we were to do that, your father would not meet your mother. You would not be born of them, nor your brother Layton. All things about you and your family would not exist. That is the only way."

Raising up on his toes with outstretched arms, MarlonDale said, "I would rather not be, than to bear this responsibility."

Terry reached into Alton's waistband and grabbed the Glock. He rose from their huddle and stood erect. He spoke calmly.

"I understand what needs to be done," Terry said as he put the barrel to his temple and pulled the trigger.

Chapter 61

Terry flinched. Nothing happened.

Alton stood quickly and grabbed the pistol from Dr. Hendershat's hand.

"I don't keep a round in the chamber until I am ready to shoot," Alton said. "Gun safety 101, Dr. H."

One by one, they each stood, immersed in fear and fascination.

The Host spoke for all to hear.

"The son is ready to give his life for the father, the father is ready to give his life for the son, each willing to give their lives for their world," the Host said. "Oh, so refreshing, almost Mercurian. Fascinating, just wonderful. Humans, so inspiring at times, yet so recalcitrant and stiff-necked, almost Mercurian. Then it shall be rewritten."

"So, what shall be rewritten?" Alton, the pragmatistic sociopath, asked.

A silvery, translucent cloud burst from the ground in front of the group. The Host appeared on the mound to answer Alton.

"The now, the future, that is what will be rewritten," the Host said. "And it will start immediately."

The Host hovered in the middle of the circle, silently communicating to all of them.

"My dear Alton, using your skill sets, you will completely destroy Dr. Hendershat's Virotics Lab," the Host said. "There will be nothing left with which a Virotic Vaccine can be produced. Complete destruction, and I would like you to do this on a Sunday to keep the collateral damage minimal. I have faith in your certain abilities for good and evil. "

Alton smiled and said, "Alton like."

"Many of your people will die from the coming pandemic, it is coming. I will not stop it," the Host said. "Terry and McAllister, you will use your healing abilities and talents during the recovery process. Your species will return to the land, and you will be better stewards for this planet in the coming years, for the Mercurians and your own sake.

The Host addressed Marlon.

"And you, Marlon, MarlonDale Hendershat," the Host said. "Well, we are a generation behind, but how much do you know about Geo-Biology and JB Weld?" The Host smiled.

Marlon smiled, too.

2053726R00149

Made in the USA
San Bernardino, CA
06 March 2013